The morning air was cool and crisp—the kind
of fall morning that tingled against your skin
and made your breath curl in soft clouds. A
gentle breeze stirred the amber leaves along
the sidewalk, sending them tumbling like
confetti across the school's freshly trimmed
lawn. The rich, earthy scent of damp soil
mingled with the unmistakable aroma of freshly
cut grass, while the distant hum of lawn
mowers buzzed rhythmically behind the school,
like the low purring of giant insects.

Golden light spilled lazily over the front
entrance as the sun peeked above the horizon,
casting long shadows across the concrete. The
sky was painted in soft blues and tangerine
oranges, a picture-perfect backdrop for the
start of another school day.

Elizabeth Kane stood at her usual spot near
the gate, her silhouette crisp and poised
against the morning glow. Her heels clicked
with practiced rhythm against the pavement—
each step precise, confident, and commanding.
She was a portrait of composure and quiet
authority.

Her dirty blonde hair was swept back into a
sleek ponytail that gleamed in the sunlight, not
a single strand out of place. Hazel eyes, sharp

and intelligent, scanned the crowd beneath meticulously shaped brows. A faint trail of freckles dusted the bridge of her nose, softening the sharpness of her cheekbones. Her fitted ivory blouse hugged her frame beneath a gray wool coat, neatly tucked into tailored navy slacks. Pearl studs shimmered faintly beneath her hair, and the soft beige of her lipstick completed the look—elegant, composed, and utterly in control.

But beneath the polish, there was a quiet grit to her—something unspoken but palpable. The kind of edge that came from long nights, hard calls, and learning to read between the lines of what people said and what they meant. Elizabeth Kane didn't just manage a school— she *studied* it. She saw the subtle shifts in tone, the darting eyes, the clenched jaws. She knew when something wasn't right.

And this morning, something wasn't right.

"Morning, Marcus. Sharp haircut," she called out with a warm grin, her voice smooth and engaging.

The boy blinked in surprise, then grinned sheepishly as he ran a hand over his newly buzzed hair.

"Hey Jazmine! That yellow jacket is giving sunshine today."

The students responded with smiles, nods, and the occasional shy wave. Elizabeth meant every word. This wasn't a performance. This was part of her rhythm—making sure every student felt *seen* before they ever made it to first period.

But as the wave of students slowed, a ripple of unease stirred beneath her calm exterior.

When she stepped into the front office, the scent of coffee and disinfectant hit her nose, but the instinct in her gut spoke louder for some reason today.

And then she saw Miss Karen.

Karen was usually sunshine in human form—round-cheeked, always smiling, with warm brown eyes and a laugh that could brighten even the darkest Monday. Today, though, her face was drawn tight, lips pressed into a thin line, and her eyes were too wide—too anxious.

Her curly black hair, usually pulled back into a cheerful ponytail with a colorful scrunchie, was slightly frizzed, like she'd been running her fingers through it too often. She wore a cardigan covered in little pumpkins, but the festive warmth of her outfit couldn't hide the worry in her posture.

Elizaboth raiood an oyobrow and gooturod gently. "Come in," she said, already bracing herself.

Inside her office, the quiet buzz of a lawn mower outside gave the illusion of calm. But Elizabeth was already on alert.

Karen sat carefully, wringing her hands in her lap—something Elizabeth had only seen once before, years ago, when a student had revealed something truly awful.

"I'm worried about Craig," Karen said, her voice low and tight.

Elizabeth blinked, then nodded slowly, setting aside the discipline referral she'd been reviewing. "How can I help?"

Outwardly, she was calm—every movement measured, her posture straight. But inside?

Her stomach twisted.

Craig.

Craig wasn't a behavior problem. If anything, he was the opposite—a wide-eyed, slow-moving, sweet-hearted boy with a constant smudge on his cheek and an eagerness to please. He had a round face, too small for his oversized hoodie, with eyes that looked just a little bit lost most of the time. His brown hair was thick and messy, curling in clumps at the back like he'd slept on the floor.

He often spoke in fragmented sentences and had trouble following conversations, but his heart was gold. He didn't argue. He didn't lie. He didn't *steal.*

Until now.

"He's been coming to school in the same clothes every day," Karen said, voice trembling slightly. "They're getting worse. His hair is matted. His body odor is…" she paused, "…overwhelming."

Elizabeth's face remained composed, but her hands curled slightly against her desk.

"And this morning," Karen continued, "he took another student's sandwich. And when the student got upset, Craig didn't understand why."

Elizabeth knew this story.

She had lived it—too many times.

Kids stealing food because there wasn't any at home. Kids who didn't get why other kids were upset because their brains had never fully developed social understanding. Kids who said things like—

"He told me he can see the stars when he goes to sleep."

And there it was.

Elizabeth's heart dropped straight to her shoes.

She stayed still, but inside her mind was racing.

Sleeping outside. Probably in a tent. Maybe a car. Maybe not even that.

She nodded slowly. "I'll check our records. See if we have any updated information."

Karen nodded, but her eyes stayed locked on Elizabeth's. "Should we report it to CPS?"

Elizabeth hesitated.

Not because she didn't know the answer. But because she *did.*

And the answer was *bullshit.*

"We'll document everything," she said softly, diplomatically. "Let's try to find out more before we call."

Translation: *They won't lift a finger unless he's bruised or bleeding.*

By the end of the day, she had combed through every document, every number, every address.

Nothing.

Disconnected.

Invalid.

Useless.

The only consistent thread?

Craig's mother still picked him up after school.

So Elizabeth waited.

She stood near the gate again, the sky now blushing pink as the sun dipped lower behind the school. The smell of fresh grass still lingered in the air, though now mixed with the faint scent of exhaust from the departing school buses.

And then she saw him.

Craig trudged toward the curb, his backpack dragging low behind him, his sweatshirt stained at the sleeves. His shoes looked too small— one sole peeling at the front, flapping with each step like a broken mouth.

And then came his mother.

Gaunt. Pale. Her face sallow beneath smudges of old makeup, lips chapped and jaw set tight. She looked like someone who had lost a fight she hadn't even realized she was in.

Elizabeth had seen mothers like this before—women clinging to survival, doing the bare minimum just to get through the day. But was it neglect, or was it exhaustion? Was there a version of this woman's life where she had enough money, enough support, where Craig had a bed and a full stomach?

Maybe.

But that version wasn't here.

Here, she was just another mother failing her kid.

Her eyes darted around, too quick, too paranoid. Her jeans were threadbare, her jacket unzipped despite the chill in the air. She straddled a bicycle with rusted handlebars and bent spokes, waving him over with one long, bony arm.

No car. No house key. No clear destination.

Just a bicycle.

Elizabeth stood motionless, face unreadable.

But inside?

She burned.

Not this time, she thought.

Not Craig.

Not if she could fucking help it.

Two

The sky had shifted into a pale, overcast gray by late morning, casting a cool, moody hue over the school grounds. The golden light from earlier had faded, leaving the campus bathed in silvery shadows and the soft rustle of wind.

Inside the main office, the air was still, sterile, and faintly buzzing with fluorescent light. The walls were lined with safety posters and outdated announcements, all slightly curled at the corners.

Elizabeth Kane sat at her desk, eyes fixed on her screen, back straight as a rod, fingers rhythmically tapping on the wood in front of her. Her coffee mug sat untouched near her elbow. She'd intended to drink it this morning, but one sniff had told her everything she needed to know.

Cinnamon.

Someone—probably Linda—had added cinnamon to the staff coffee again.

Elizabeth didn't need to taste it. She could smell that spicy, over-eager note floating in the air like a Hallmark movie trying too hard. It clung to the office like it belonged there. It didn't.

Ruined again, she muttered inwardly.

She liked her coffee *normal*: strong, smooth, and drowned in hazelnut creamer—the kind that gave just enough sweetness to balance out the bitterness of her long mornings. This cinnamon crap tasted like somebody melted a scented candle into the pot. She pushed the mug farther away.

Her attention returned to the blinking cursor on her screen—the CPS reporting portal.

She had filled these out before. Hundreds of times. But this one weighed heavier. The system always demanded something more. Something worse.

She took a breath and began typing.

> The Report
> "Student appears to be experiencing homelessness. Has come to school in the same clothes for multiple days. Hygiene concerns are increasing. Student has been stealing food from peers. Teacher reports student mentioned 'seeing the stars at night when he sleeps.' Guardian has no working phone, and addresses on file are outdated. Concerned for student's well-being and access to basic needs."

She hovered, rereading the words. It didn't feel like enough—not to reflect what she *knew* was happening.

Then she picked up the phone and dialed the direct CPS intake number.

The line clicked.
"Child Protective Services. This is Renee."

Elizabeth cleared her throat. "I'm calling to report a student. I submitted a written report, but I wanted to provide context. His name is Craig Tucker."

She laid it all out: the same unwashed clothes, the visible decline in hygiene, the reports of food theft, the cognitive delays. She described how he mentioned "seeing stars" when he slept.

Then Renee sighed, clearly annoyed. "Ma'am, I'm not sure why you're calling this in. You're saying the child has dirty hair and hasn't showered? That's not abuse."

Elizabeth pressed her fingers into her temple. "He's been in the same clothes for over a week. He smells like he hasn't bathed in longer than that. He's stealing food because he's hungry. He told a teacher he sleeps *outside.*"

"Well," Renee said, "parents take their kids camping all the time. Sleeping outdoors isn't abuse."

Elizabeth blinked. *Camping?* This woman thought Craig was *camping?*

Her voice dropped lower, sharper. "He is cognitively delayed. He can't articulate what's happening."

"Do you have documentation of abuse? Medical records? A statement from the child?"

"No," Elizabeth snapped. "Because I'm not a detective. I'm a school administrator. It's *your job* to investigate suspected neglect."

Another sigh on the line. "Unless you can confirm he's actually homeless—"

"He's being picked up from school *on a bicycle.*"

Silence.

Then, with bureaucratic indifference: "If you obtain additional information, you're welcome to submit another report."

Elizabeth's jaw tightened. "What's your name?"

"...Renee Jackson."

She wrote it down.

"Perfect. Have a great day, Renee."

Click.

The phone slammed down.

Elizabeth sat in silence, the edges of her vision tinged with heat. She stared at the wall for a long second. Her pen was still in her hand. Her jaw ached from clenching.

Craig was still out there—vulnerable, cold, and invisible to the people who were supposed to protect him.

If the system wouldn't help him…
She would.

Elizabeth didn't waste time.

She grabbed her radio and keyed it. "Smith, you in your office?"

The reply crackled back almost instantly. "Always. Come on in."

She left the building, the wind hitting her full in the face as she crossed the open walkway. Leaves scattered in her path, and the sky had taken on a deep pewter hue. The day felt heavy now. Expectant.

Inside Officer Smith's small office, it was warmer—but only barely. The space heater in the corner buzzed like a dying insect, and the room smelled like old paperwork and cheap roast coffee... with that same damn cinnamon twist.

Elizabeth wrinkled her nose. *Fucking Linda.*

Smith sat behind his cluttered desk, legs stretched out, sipping from a chipped mug that read World's Okayest Cop. He was enormous—well over six-foot-three—and thick through the middle, built like a teddy bear in a bulletproof vest. His shaved head shone under the overhead light, but you could still see the shadow of what used to be a hairline—the seedlings of recession stubbornly clinging to their territory.

He had the kind of face that was always smiling, even when he wasn't. Laugh lines crinkled around his eyes, and a kind of jolly calmness followed him like a warm breeze. He was one of Elizabeth's favorites—steady, reliable, and real. He worked hard, treated kids with respect, and always showed up.

He just... really loved donuts. And his genes had betrayed him when it came to hair.

Still, she wouldn't trade him for ten officers in pressed uniforms and zero personality.

"Bad day?" he asked, his voice like gravel mixed with honey.

"Craig Tucker," she said simply.

His smile faded. "What's going on?"

She filled him in—fast, sharp, and unfiltered. CPS's apathy. Craig's worsening condition. The stars.

Smith didn't interrupt. He just nodded, then turned to his computer and started typing.

"This is a mess," he muttered. "His first listed address—316 G Street? Doesn't exist."

Elizabeth crossed her arms. "Fake?"

"Yeah. Doesn't show up on any city record. Second one—417 Atterbury Court—got flagged for eviction last month."

She felt her jaw clench again.

"And this one," Smith said darkly, pointing to the screen. "This one's a problem."

111 Ellen Court, Apartment 7C.

She didn't even need him to say it. That was *the* street. The one you circled in red ink. A known pocket for offenders, addicts, and ghosts.

Smith pulled up the record.

"John Dale," he said. "Registered sex offender. Multiple counts. All involving minors."

Elizabeth closed her eyes, then opened them slowly. "How long were Craig and his mother there?"

"Long enough," he said quietly.

Her throat tightened. She nodded once. "Can you talk to him? Dale?"

Smith pushed back from his desk and stood. "On it."

Elizabeth walked briskly back to her office, her coat flapping behind her like a cape. The sky outside had grown darker, and the wind pressed against the windows like a warning.

She didn't even sit. She just marched to her computer and filed a second CPS report— fingers flying.

> "Additional information regarding Craig Tucker's possible homelessness. Last confirmed address was with a registered sex offender, John Dale. Family has since left that location and cannot be found. Student may be in danger."

She fed the paper into the fax machine.

The old machine whined in protest, as if it resented having to do its job.

She waited.

And waited.

The office was silent now, save for the rhythmic groaning of the heater and the occasional gust of wind rattling the windowpanes. The cinnamon smell had finally begun to fade, replaced by the dry, faintly dusty scent of warm electronics and anxiety.

By the time the phone rang, the sun had dipped fully below the horizon. Her office was bathed in artificial light, throwing long shadows across the floor.

She snatched up the receiver. "Kane."

The voice on the other end was cold and robotic. "Thank you for your report. We'll investigate when possible."

Elizabeth closed her eyes. "This child is homeless. He was living with a convicted pedophile."

A pause.

"We don't have the resources right now. If you get more information, let us know."

Click.

The line went dead.

Elizabeth stared at the receiver in her hand,
her mind quiet but her body shaking with rage.

Craig was still out there. Hungry. Cold.
Unprotected.

And no one was coming.

No one but her.

Three

Elizabeth Kane didn't believe in waiting around. Not for people. Not for paperwork. And sure as hell not for broken systems that left kids like Craig Tucker sleeping outside.

If no one else was going to find him, then she would.

She didn't know where he was sleeping, but she knew one thing: every day, like clockwork, Craig's mother picked him up on that damn rusted bicycle. No car. No bus pass. Just a cracked frame with squeaky brakes and an overstuffed wire basket that held more weight than it ever should've.

And today, Elizabeth was going to follow them.

But first, she needed a plan.

Her office was quiet, the fluorescent lights above humming faintly as the wind outside rattled against the windows. The smell of cinnamon coffee still clung stubbornly to the air—sweet and offensive.

Elizabeth leaned back in her chair and grabbed her radio.

"Mateo. Ashley. My office. Now."

Less than five minutes later, Mateo Tomas waltzed in first, sipping a lavender iced coffee with extra foam and a green straw.

"Yoo-hoo. You rang?" he said, his voice dripping with sass and curiosity.

Ashley Franks came in right behind him, clipboard in hand and an eyebrow already halfway raised. "This isn't about Craig, is it?"

Elizabeth didn't answer right away. She steepled her fingers, leaned back in her chair, and crossed her legs with all the theatrical pause of a Bond villain.

"I need to find out where Craig is staying. The system won't help, so I'm going to follow him after school. But I need him to move slow enough for me to keep up—without being obvious."

Mateo blinked. "Are you about to say something illegal?"

"No," Elizabeth replied. "Just… morally flexible."

Mateo perked up. "Oh. My favorite flavor."

Ashley groaned. "Elizabeth… don't tell me you're planning to mess with his bike."

Elizabeth lifted a single eyebrow.

Ashley slapped a hand to her forehead. "Oh, God."

"It's just air, Ashley. I'm not slashing his tires. I just need to deflate one a little—just enough to slow them down."

"That's exactly the kind of thing people get fired for," Ashley muttered.

"Only if you get caught," Mateo added, unhelpfully.

Elizabeth smirked. "Relax. It'll be fast. Subtle. He'll still be able to ride—just a little slower. I'll follow on foot."

Mateo leaned against the filing cabinet, grinning. "You know, I always suspected you had a tiny criminal streak under all those pearls."

Elizabeth's smirk deepened. "Oh, you're going to love this."

That afternoon, the sky had clouded over again. A soft breeze tugged at the corners of papers clipped to student folders. A leaf or two skittered across the concrete as the final bell rang and students poured out like a slow, chattering wave.

Elizabeth positioned herself at the gates, clipboard in hand, her professional mask firmly in place.

Craig stood by the bike rack, dragging his oversized backpack across the ground and stuffing it into the rattling basket on the front of his mother's ancient bicycle. She wasn't there yet.

Perfect.

Elizabeth strolled toward the rack, the confident *click-click* of her stiletto heels echoing across the pavement. She smiled at students as they passed, nodding at a few parents, all while casually sidling up next to the rusted bike like it was just another part of her end-of-day rounds.

Then—fluid as ever—she adjusted her heel, dropped her weight slightly, and gently pressed her stiletto against the tire valve.

Hisssssssss.

Air escaped in a slow, barely audible stream. Elizabeth kept her eyes up, chatting with a student about the upcoming spirit week as the tire quietly deflated beneath her foot.

Thirty seconds. Done.

She turned and strolled back toward the gate just as Craig's mother arrived. She looked just as exhausted as the bike—hollow-cheeked, eyes sunken, one pant leg torn at the hem. Her tangled hair was barely contained in a stretched-out scrunchie.

"Come on," she called.

Craig groaned. "Mom, the tire's flat!"

His mother squinted, then cursed under her breath. "Damn tire…"

She shook her head, dismounted, and grabbed the handlebars. "We'll have to walk. Let's go."

Elizabeth turned and walked the opposite way, a quiet smile tugging at the corner of her lips.

Now we're getting somewhere.

She followed them from a distance, careful to pause at corners, pretend to scroll through her phone, and cross when cars passed to avoid drawing attention. Her heels echoed against the sidewalk, sharp and precise.

And then it happened.

The very sidewalk slab beneath her betrayed her.

Her stiletto sank into a crack.

She pulled—once, twice—then yanked.

SNAP.

The heel broke clean off.

Elizabeth stumbled forward like a wounded gazelle, flailed slightly, and nearly collided with a trash can. Her clipboard clattered to the pavement.

"Oh, for fuck's sake," she muttered.

People turned to look.

And worst of all—Craig's mother turned, too.

Elizabeth froze, pretending to check a text on her phone… which, unfortunately, was upside down.

Craig's mom squinted, eyebrows knit together.

Elizabeth gave her best *don't-mind-me-I'm-just-a-normal-citizen* smile.

After a long, uncomfortable pause, Craig's mom turned back around.

Elizabeth exhaled slowly. *Crisis averted.*

She bent down to retrieve her clipboard, now wobbling slightly, with one heel broken and the other defiantly intact, clicking unevenly on the concrete.

And that was when the dog showed up.

He trotted out from behind a pile of soggy cardboard boxes like he owned the sidewalk— a scrappy little mutt with matted tan fur and a black patch over one eye.

Elizabeth stopped in her tracks.

It was that dog.

The one from The Little Rascals.

She'd hated that movie her entire life.

The moment she saw that stupid black eye patch and wiry body waddling toward her like he was the damn mayor of Sad Town, a deep-rooted fury surged up from somewhere in her childhood.

She had despised The Little Rascals with every fiber of her being—the cloying tone, the overdone "aww shucks" cuteness, the weird names like Spanky and Alfalfa, and worst of all, that kid with the greased-up hair and squeaky little cartoon voice, belting out that stupid love song with his toothy grin and bug eyes like a ventriloquist dummy that came to life.

Elizabeth had spent the entire movie as a kid seething, wondering why adults found it charming that a bunch of under-supervised children ran around in suits acting like middle-aged divorcees in a community theater production.

And now, somehow, life had manifested that exact little bastard of a dog in front of her.

He had the same smug little strut. The same ridiculous patch. The same unearned charm.

Of course it's you, she thought bitterly.

The mutt trotted up to her like they were old friends. He wagged his tail, looked her dead in the eyes, and—

"Oh, don't you dare—"

He sniffed.

Then lifted his leg.

"You are not serious—"

Warmth hit her ankle like betrayal.

She gasped, stumbling backward as the tiny beast peed—peed!—on her foot like she was a goddamn fire hydrant.

He gave a satisfied shake of his back leg, then strutted away, tail wagging like he'd just solved world peace.

Elizabeth stood there in complete disbelief.

She blinked once. Twice. Her mouth slightly open. Her heel soaked.

That dog—that fucking dog—had just marked her like territory.

Her eye twitched.

"That little shit," she muttered. "You flea-infested, candle-sniffing, fucking disgrace—"

She yanked a tissue from her purse and wiped at her ankle furiously, trying not to gag as the acrid smell hit her nose.

"I have a master's degree," she hissed to no one in particular. "I graduated summa cum laude. I once gave a presentation to the state superintendent. I do not deserve this."

But here she was. Limiting her speed-walk to a limp, a broken stiletto in one hand, and a pee-slicked ankle on the other.

She gave her foot one last aggressive shake in the grass, stood up straight, clenched her jaw, and marched forward.

She was not quitting now.

Not for the system.
Not for the stupid movie dog.
And definitely not for Alfalfa's weird little love ballad.

They walked for miles it seemed.

Elizabeth trailed them like a shadow, ducking behind signs and parked cars when needed, still wobbling slightly and now carrying the unmistakable scent of "pee, disappointment, and cinnamon coffee."

They passed shuttered businesses, graffiti-tagged dumpsters, and empty lots filled with broken-down cars and forgotten belongings. This was the edge of town. The part people drove past with their windows up.

And then—they stopped.

Craig's mother pushed open a bent chain-link fence behind a gas station, and led him through an overgrown lot filled with discarded tires and plastic bags caught in tree branches.

A small, battered tent sat near the back corner, hidden between two dumpsters and an old billboard that read YOU ARE LOVED in chipped, faded paint.

Clothes were piled in trash bags next to the tent. A milk crate held a few water bottles and cans of food. Craig ducked inside without a word.

His mother stayed outside and lit a cigarette with hands that trembled from more than the cold.

Elizabeth stood frozen on the sidewalk across the street.

This wasn't camping.
 This was survival.

They were living here.

Her chest tightened.

The anger returned—low and fierce in her gut.

The system had failed him. Just like she knew it would.

But now she had seen it. With her own eyes.

There was no turning back.

She turned away, limping slightly, her broken heel clicking awkwardly against the pavement.

The sun was nearly gone now, the sky darkening into a wash of slate blue and ash gray.

She had a cigarette-scented ankle, a broken shoe, and half a plan.

But she also had proof.

And that meant she had *work to do*.

Four

The sky was ink-black and heavy with coastal fog as Elizabeth Kane sat alone in her car, parked a block away from the dimly lit gas station. The streetlight above flickered lazily, casting long, ghostlike shadows across the cracked pavement. A half-empty soda cup rolled in a lazy arc down the curb, pushed by the wind like it, too, had nowhere better to be.

The lot beyond her windshield was quiet, save for the low, rhythmic hum of a nearby vending machine and the faint buzz of a faulty neon "OPEN" sign that pulsed like a weak heartbeat in the window of the gas station store. Behind it, half-hidden by overgrown weeds and a sagging wooden fence, sat the tent.

A battered dome of blue nylon and duct tape. A home.

Elizabeth's hands were curled into fists in her lap, her nails digging crescents into her skin. Her heart wasn't pounding from fear. It wasn't adrenaline.

It was rage.

Craig was living in a damn tent.

A child.

A cognitively delayed child who needed warmth, structure, food—safety. Instead, he was curled up on the cold ground, sleeping behind a gas station while the system that claimed to protect him sat behind locked office doors, safe and warm.

She'd done everything right. Reported. Documented. Followed the damn procedure.

And what did CPS tell her?

Dirty hair isn't reportable.
Stealing food isn't proof of neglect.
It's not your job to investigate.

Well.

She had investigated.

And now, as the cold air from her slightly cracked window wrapped around her neck like a warning, she thought only one thing:

If they won't help him, I will.

She took a slow breath, trying to steady her pulse and think clearly.

What was the next move?

Pictures. Documentation. Something undeniable. Craig's word wouldn't be enough—

he couldn't explain his circumstances. His mother would deny everything. CPS needed something physical. Visual.

Proof.

She clenched the steering wheel, her knuckles whitening against the leather grip.

Fine. If they wanted proof, she'd get it.

Her phone buzzed on the passenger seat, the vibration rattling softly against the cracked vinyl upholstery. She glanced down, expecting another hollow email from a case worker.

But it was Mateo.

> MATEO: Don't forget about your dinner date, queen. Gentleman Caller #4 awaits.

Shit.

Rick.

She had completely forgotten. Again.

Rick: the nice, average-looking guy she'd met at a district fundraiser. Clean-cut. Steady job. Drives a Toyota and listens to Coldplay unironically.

He wasn't a bad guy.

He just wasn't *her* guy even though he wanted to be.

Still… the sex was decent. Actually, better than decent when she'd had a couple drinks and let her mind slow down long enough to enjoy it.

Her choice of drink usually determined her mood.

Pinot Noir? Slow, seductive, meaningful eye contact.
 Lemon drop? Light, flirty, maybe a little giggly.
 Tequila? That was *rough day* energy. Quick, desperate, and unfiltered.

Tonight?

She wasn't even sure what category she belonged in.

> ELIZABETH: Fuck. I forgot. Tell him I'm running late.

> MATEO: Already did. But if you ghost this man again, I'm telling him you're into taxidermy roleplay and had second thoughts.

> ELIZABETH: You're the worst.

> MATEO: And yet, you love me.

Elizabeth rolled her eyes and tossed the phone onto the passenger seat. She started the car and shifted into drive.

The restaurant was warm and softly lit, all Edison bulbs and reclaimed wood—trying very hard to be romantic but still one Yelp star short of impressive. Jazz played through overhead speakers, too quiet to notice unless you listened, but annoying once you did.

Elizabeth walked in, thirty minutes late, her heels echoing against the polished concrete floor. Her coat still smelled faintly of exhaust and frustration.

Rick was already seated at a table near the window, his shoulders stiff, posture polite. A glass of Pinot Noir waited in front of her place setting, the stem shining like it had something to prove.

She sighed.

Not fucking happening.

Sliding into the seat across from him, she offered a practiced smile. "Sorry. Work ran long."

Rick smiled back, the kind of smile that didn't quite reach his eyes. "No problem. I ordered you the Pinot."

She picked it up, gave it a swirl, took a single polite sip, and immediately set it down. The taste felt heavy in her mouth—like a promise she didn't want to keep.

Rick noticed. The mood shifted.

He tried, bless him. Made small talk. Laughed at his own jokes. Told a story about a coworker who microwaved salmon in the break room.

But Elizabeth couldn't hear him.

All she could see was Craig.

Cold. Hungry. Lying on a nylon floor behind a gas station while the rest of the world ordered wine and pretended not to know.

Rick reached for her hand. She pulled hers back, fingers tightening against her palm like a reflex she couldn't unlearn. "You okay?" he asked, his voice quiet, cautious.

She almost laughed at the question. Was she okay? Craig was dead. His mother was dead. And somewhere in a police report, their deaths would be summed up in three lines of text while the drunk driver who hit them slept off a hangover.

She should go home. Sleep. Process.

But the idea of sitting alone in her house, listening to the quiet, made her stomach turn.

"I have an early morning," she said, voice smooth, the lie effortless. Then she leaned in, just enough that Rick would misread the tension in her body as something he could fix. "But not that early."

Rick said he understood.

But his disappointment was louder than anything he said aloud.

Elizabeth tossed a few bills on the table and didn't touch her wine again. As she walked away, she could feel his eyes on her back. That was probably the last she'd hear from him.

Good.

Because right now, she didn't need wine. Or sex. Or someone who couldn't possibly understand her world.

She needed action.

She didn't go home.

Instead, she drove across town to Ashley's tiny stucco house nestled on a quiet street of overwatered lawns and solar garden lights. The neighborhood smelled like lavender dryer sheets and wood smoke.

Ashley opened the door in sweatpants, an oversized hoodie, and a wine glass bigger than her face. "What now?" she asked, already stepping aside.

Elizabeth walked past her without hesitation. "Craig and his mother are living behind a gas station. In a tent."

Ashley blinked. "...Jesus."

"I need proof," Elizabeth said, turning sharply to face her. "CPS isn't moving. If we don't document this, nothing's going to happen."

Ashley stared at her. "You want me to go take pictures of a child's tent? While he's *in* it?"

"Yes."

Ashley rubbed her temples like the conversation was giving her a migraine. "Elizabeth..."

"Ashley." Her voice was steel. "You heard what they said. You heard that woman. If we don't bring them something undeniable, Craig stays out there until something worse happens."

Ashley exhaled through her nose and shook her head, then grabbed her sweatshirt off the back of a chair. "Fine. But if I get arrested—"

"I'll bail you out," Elizabeth said instantly.

Ashley gave her a look. "That was *way* too fast."

Elizabeth shrugged. "You've seen my record. Boundaries and I have a complicated relationship."

Ashley groaned. "Yeah. No shit."

The next morning, a gray drizzle coated the school parking lot in a sheet of fine mist. Students huddled under backpacks and hoodies, darting between awnings as early traffic backed up outside the front gate.

Elizabeth sat at her desk, perfectly still, phone in hand, photos from Ashley open on her screen.

There was the tent.
The trash bags.
The gas station sign in the background.
The date.
The timestamp.

Undeniable.

She pressed "Call."

The phone rang twice.

"Child Protective Services, how can I help you?"

"This is Elizabeth Kane, Associate Principal at Shore Ridge High School," she began, her voice clipped. "I submitted a report for Craig Tucker. It was denied. I now have photo evidence that he is living behind a gas station. I am reporting this again—under neglect and endangerment."

The woman on the other end sighed. "Ma'am, as I explained last time—"

Elizabeth cut her off. "What's your name?"

A pause.

"Excuse me?"

"Your name. For my records. Since I'll be escalating this to the district and to our local media partners."

Silence.

Elizabeth didn't blink.

Finally, the woman stammered, "I—I'll transfer you to a supervisor."

Elizabeth leaned back, her smile ice-cold.

Gotcha.

By the end of the day, CPS had agreed to send someone out.

It didn't mean Craig was safe. It didn't mean justice had arrived. It didn't mean the world had suddenly remembered how to care.

But it meant Elizabeth had forced them to look.

She had forced them to listen.

And if they ever dared ignore him again?

She'd be waiting.

Because Elizabeth Kane didn't back down.

And she wasn't losing this fight.

Not now.
 Not ever.

Five

Elizabeth was deep in sleep, limbs twisted in a heap of cotton sheets, her mouth slightly open, breath slow and steady. Her bedroom was still, blanketed in predawn shadows, the faintest glow of morning light just beginning to creep through the window blinds.

Then came the weight.

A solid, purring lump settled squarely on her chest.

A low, rhythmic rumble vibrated through her ribcage.

Then—*thump-thump-thump*—soft paws kneading right into her sternum.

Zeus.

Her asshole cat.

Making himself perfectly at home.

Right on top of her phone.

She groaned, one eye cracking open as a muffled buzz sounded from beneath his furry bulk. Zeus blinked at her, entirely unbothered. She shoved him off with a grunt, and he flopped to the floor like a judgmental potato.

Elizabeth squinted at the screen.

5:30 AM.

One text.

MR. SCHWARTZ: Are you awake?

Her stomach tightened.

That was never a good sign.

She rubbed her eyes and sat up slowly, the air in the room cold against her skin. Her feet hit the hardwood floor, cool and smooth as she shuffled toward the window, brushing aside the curtain to stare out at the still-dark morning. Streetlamps buzzed faintly outside. A sprinkler sputtered to life in a neighbor's yard.

Her house was quiet. Too quiet.

It always was.

A clean, modern space with cold colors and sharp edges. No personal touches. No soft pastels. No baby pictures or family photos. Just functionality. A fortress designed to keep emotion at bay.

The second bedroom? A gym. Punching bag. Squat rack. Rowing machine.
The third? A work cave. Stacks of paperwork. A whiteboard scrawled with upcoming events, interventions, and goal charts.

There was no guest room. No nursery. No space carved out for what might have been.

Sometimes, in the quieter hours of the night, she wondered what it would feel like to have someone. A husband. A kid. A golden retriever curled up by the fire.

But those thoughts never lasted long.

She had chosen her path. And her mission wasn't domestic bliss.

It was her kids.

All 2,500 of them.

She picked up her phone and texted back.

> ELIZABETH: El Jefe, you're up early.

The response came almost immediately.

> MR. SCHWARTZ: Call me.

Her stomach twisted.

Schwartz never asked for a call unless it was serious.

She took a breath, braced herself, and hit dial.

The line connected after one ring.

"Morning, boss," she said, her voice rough from sleep but steady.

Schwartz's voice came through, low and heavy.

"Craig's dead."

The words didn't register at first.

Elizabeth blinked. Her throat went dry.

"What?" she whispered.

"A drunk driver," Schwartz said quietly. "Officer Smith will give you the full report when he gets in. I didn't want you to hear it secondhand."

Silence.

Elizabeth stood frozen, the phone pressed against her ear. She felt like she was underwater. Numb. Disconnected. Her vision tunneled.

She tried to speak, but her tongue was a rock in her mouth.

Finally—mechanically—she said, "I'll be in soon."

"Elizabeth—" Schwartz began, but—

Click.

She hung up.

She moved on autopilot.

Shower. Hair. Makeup. Clothes.

Each action disconnected from her body, as if she were watching someone else go through the motions. Her reflection stared back at her in the bathroom mirror—blank, pale, composed. A ghost in eyeliner.

She dried her hair half-heartedly, left it down, didn't care. Threw on black slacks and a blouse. No jewelry. No lipstick. Just her armor.

She grabbed her keys, slipped her phone into her bag, and stepped into her boots instead of heels.

Today wasn't a heels day.

Today was war.

Before leaving, she paused at the door, resting her hand on the knob.

Craig is dead.

She whispered it aloud.

Her chest clenched.

I will never let this happen again.

The sky was still waking up when Elizabeth pulled into the staff lot. The asphalt gleamed with a thin sheen of morning dew. Her boots hit the pavement hard as she marched across the lot and pushed through the front doors.

The air inside the school was warmer but stale, humming with quiet fluorescent lighting and early-morning stillness.

She turned toward the staff lounge, needing one small moment to regroup before she faced the full weight of the day.

And that was when it hit her.

The smell.

Cinnamon.

That overly sweet, over-seasoned, artificially cozy scent hit her like a punch to the face.

Someone—probably fucking Linda—had done it again. Spiked the staff coffee with that goddamn cinnamon creamer like she was hosting a holiday brunch in hell.

Elizabeth stalked to the coffee pot, yanked it from the burner, and dumped the entire thing down the sink. The hot liquid gurgled, splashed, and hissed as it swirled away, taking its festive crime with it.

She flung open the cabinet, found the offending bottle of "Saigon Cinnamon", and held it up like it was evidence in a murder trial.

Without hesitation, she threw it straight into the trash can and slammed the lid shut.

Just as she turned around, Mateo appeared in the doorway, sipping his signature iced lavender latte, eyebrows raised.

"Jesus," he said. "Rough morning?"

Elizabeth glared at him. "Do not start."

Mateo, wisely, backed away without another word.

She took one last steadying breath.

And headed for Schwartz's office.

She shoved the door open without knocking.

Inside, Officer Smith was already seated—
massive, still, and solemn. His shaved head
caught the light from the overhead
fluorescents. Mr. Schwartz stood from behind
his desk, face lined with fatigue and sadness.

"Sit down," Schwartz said gently.

Elizabeth didn't.

"Tell me," she demanded.

Smith exhaled.

"Report came in just after 2 a.m. Drunk driver
lost control, flipped their vehicle, and plowed
through the empty lot behind the gas station.
Craig and his mother were inside their tent."

Elizabeth felt her knees go weak.

No.

No, no, no, no.

"They both died at the scene," Smith
continued, his voice stripped of emotion.
"Didn't even make it to the hospital."

She couldn't breathe.

Her hands curled into fists, her nails digging
into her palms.

"And the driver?" she asked.

Smith glanced down. "Minor injuries. Walked away."

Elizabeth's jaw snapped shut. Her heart thundered in her ears.

Then—her voice exploded.

"Are you *fucking kidding me?!*"

The words cracked through the room like thunder.

Smith didn't flinch.

Schwartz didn't blink.

Because they knew.

Because *they felt it too.*

The gut-wrenching injustice of it all. That a child—*a sweet, cognitively delayed child*—was dead.

That his mother, flawed but trying, was dead.

And the drunk who ended their lives?

Scratched up. Probably sleeping it off.

Elizabeth's chest heaved, her body trembling.

The grief burned in her throat, hot and acidic, but she swallowed it down.

She wouldn't cry.

She wouldn't break.

She would *fight.*

This was it.

This was the moment.

She would never trust the system again.

Never follow the rules the same way again.

Because Craig was gone.

And no one—*no one*—had cared until it was too late.

But she would care.
And she would never let this happen again.
Even if she had to burn it all to the ground.

Six

Elizabeth moved through the day like a ghost wearing her own skin.

She was there—physically. Her boots echoed down the halls. Her clipboard was in her hand. Her smile made brief appearances where needed.

But inside?

She was somewhere else.

Somewhere colder.

Somewhere darker.

First period came and went like fog.

Elizabeth visited classrooms quietly, checking in on students who had known Craig. A few stared blankly at their desks. Others wept. Most didn't know what to feel.

Miss Karen was wrecked.

She sat at the kidney table in her classroom, her smile cracked and her posture slumped, clutching a tissue like it was the only thing holding her together. When she saw Elizabeth, she stood—then collapsed into her arms.

"I should've done more," Karen sobbed. "I should've—"

"You did everything right," Elizabeth whispered into her hair. "Everything."

But the words felt like ash in her mouth.

She checked on Ashley next.

Ashley looked like she hadn't slept. Her hair was pulled into a lazy bun. She had on one of her "I'm pretending I'm okay" outfits—tight blazer, bright lipstick, and shoes with a ridiculous heel height no sane woman would wear on a Thursday.

"You good?" Elizabeth asked quietly.

Ashley nodded too quickly. "You?"

"Yeah. I'm good."

They held each other's gaze for a long second.

Lies.

They were both lying.

But what else could they say?

The truth was too heavy for daylight hours.

By mid-morning, Elizabeth ducked into the staff lounge for a breather.

She barely made it three steps in before the scent hit her.

Fucking cinnamon. God damn it, Linda!

Again.

She stiffened.

There it was: the communal coffee pot, bubbling merrily on the counter. The steam rising from it smelled like artificial holiday cheer and bullshit.

She snapped the pot off the burner, turned, and dumped the entire thing into the sink. The hot stream hissed down the drain like it knew it was guilty.

Next, she yanked open the upper cabinet and found the plastic bottle of "Cinnamon Toast Spice" creamer, its label obnoxiously cheerful.

Elizabeth held it up.

Mateo walked in just in time to see her pitch it straight into the trash can with the force of a professional athlete.

He sipped his lavender iced coffee, eyes wide. "Wow. Cinnamon rage. It's getting worse."

"Don't push me," she muttered.

He wisely backed out of the room without another word.

By 4:00 PM, Elizabeth and Ashley were out of energy. Their smiles were cracked. Their spines ached.

Ashley tossed her keys into her purse with a sigh. "Drinks?"

Elizabeth didn't hesitate. "Patrón. No cheap shit."

They Ubered to a quiet bar on the edge of town. No TVs. No neon beer signs. Just a dim corner booth, low lighting, and the kind of silence that made you confront things you weren't ready to feel.

Elizabeth flagged down the bartender with a lift of two fingers. "Two shots of Patrón. None of that Jose Cuervo bullshit."

The bartender raised an eyebrow. "Bad experience?"

Elizabeth exhaled, her voice dry. "Jose had a tiny, dirty dick, and I don't associate with men or tequila who can't handle their shit."

Ashley choked on her water. "Jesus, Elizabeth."

The bartender outright laughed. "Fair enough."

They downed the first shot.

Then the second.

By the third, their shoulders began to relax.

By the fourth, Elizabeth's fingers felt lighter.

By the fifth, her voice dropped into a slow, fuzzy rhythm.

"What else could we have done?" Ashley asked, tracing the rim of her glass.

Elizabeth tapped her nails against the table, jaw tense. "I don't know."

Ashley didn't let her off that easy. "Yes, you do."

Elizabeth looked down at her glass. "I never want to feel this way again."

Ashley groaned softly. "That's the tequila talking."

But Elizabeth knew it wasn't.

Because *she meant it.*

Every.
Fucking.
Word.

Her phone buzzed.

She looked down, eyelids heavy, and saw a text from Rick.

He'd sent a playlist link.

The title?

"Songs That'll Make You Forget the World Exists."

She smirked.

Alcohol buzzed in her veins. Her body was humming—not from desire, not exactly—but from the need to feel something that wasn't *grief.* That wasn't *failure.*

She took a picture of the half-empty Patrón shot glass, its rim still wet with condensation, and sent it to him.

ELIZABETH: You up?

Rick responded instantly.

RICK: Uber over. I'll make you dinner.

ELIZABETH: The only thing I want for dinner is you.

A pause.

Then—

RICK: Get your ass here. Now.

The Uber dropped her off in front of Rick's townhouse—sleek, modern, sterile, like something out of a realtor's Instagram.

The second she stepped out of the car, the chill hit her legs, sharp and sobering.

But it wasn't enough to stop her.

He opened the door before she could even knock.

She didn't say hello.

She didn't need to.

Elizabeth stepped inside like a storm breaking through windows, grabbed Rick by the collar of his T-shirt, and pulled him down into a kiss that was all teeth, heat, and chaos. There was nothing gentle about it. Her fingers curled into the fabric of his shirt like claws.

Rick stumbled backward from the force of it, and Elizabeth followed, kicking the door closed with her heel.

She was already stripping her coat off, letting it fall to the floor without care, her body buzzing with tequila and adrenaline and the aching need to escape herself. Her mouth moved to his jaw, biting down just hard enough to leave a mark. She didn't want tenderness.

She wanted to *burn*.

"I need you to fuck me hard tonight," she whispered against his ear, her voice ragged and low.

Rick growled, low in his throat, his hands already locking around her thighs, lifting her like she weighed nothing. She wrapped her legs around his waist, pressing into him, feeling the hard line of his arousal already straining through his jeans.

"Jesus, Liz…"

"Don't talk," she said, her teeth grazing his bottom lip. "Just do it."

He carried her through the hallway, shouldering into the bedroom like a man possessed. She pulled his shirt over his head mid-walk, nearly taking an earring off in the process.

By the time they hit the edge of the bed, she shoved him backward and crawled onto the mattress like she owned it. Then, she flipped onto her stomach, pushing her hips up, arching her back like a fucking offering.

"Don't be soft with me," she said over her shoulder, her voice husky, firm, almost daring him.

Rick didn't hesitate.

He unbuckled his belt with a sharp snap and let it fall to the floor. His jeans followed. Then his hands were on her again—gripping her hips, running rough palms down the curve of her ass. His touch wasn't hesitant.

He *knew* what this was.

She wanted pain.
 She wanted power.
 She wanted to get lost in the sound of her own breathing.

He dragged her panties down slowly, pausing only to let his hand slip between her thighs, stroking her once—light, testing.

Sho was soakod.

He groaned behind her, his fingers digging in tighter.

"Don't tease," she warned.

And then he was inside her—*deep*—his size forcing her to grip the sheets, her mouth falling open as she gasped.

"Fuck," she hissed, pressing her forehead to the mattress, her fingers twisting in the duvet.

Rick didn't ease into it. He set a rhythm that was sharp and just as demanding as she was. Each thrust jolted through her spine, grounding her in the present, in her body, in sensation. Her grief couldn't find her here. There was no room for it.

He leaned over her, one hand braced against the bedframe, the other moving around her waist to grip her throat—not choking, just holding, grounding, controlling.

She moaned louder, pushing back into him, matching his pace.

Her hair stuck to the back of her neck, her cheeks flushed. She could feel sweat trickling down her spine, her skin tingling from the friction of his chest against her back.

Rick's free hand slid down, between her legs again—fingers finding her clit with practiced pressure. Tight, circular motions.

"Don't stop," she gasped.

He didn't.

Her legs began to tremble.

And when the orgasm hit, it was all-consuming. Her body locked up, every muscle tensing as a cry tore from her throat. It wasn't pretty. It wasn't soft.

It was *raw*.

Rick held on, riding her through it, until his own control slipped. His thrusts grew erratic, deeper, until he spilled inside her with a low, guttural curse, his body collapsing forward just enough to feel his weight press down on her, anchoring her to the bed.

For a moment, there was only the sound of their breathing. Fast. Uneven.

Then silence.

Rick moved beside her, one arm sliding under her neck. He didn't speak. Just held her.

Elizabeth lay still, eyes open, staring at the ceiling fan turning slowly above them.

Her body ached in the best way.

Her muscles were loose, her pulse slowing,
and for the first time in days, her brain wasn't
spinning in a thousand directions.

There was no Craig.
No CPS.
No fucking cinnamon coffee.

Just breath. Sweat. Silence.

Numb.

But the good kind.

Seven

Elizabeth woke up tangled in cotton sheets that weren't hers, sunlight bleeding through slatted blinds in long, precise lines across her bare legs. The room was unfamiliar—too tidy, too beige, too normal.

For a few seconds, she didn't move.

The hum of a dishwasher rumbled faintly from the kitchen. Somewhere, a ceiling fan clicked rhythmically. A bird chirped outside the window like it was mocking her for still being in bed at—she glanced at the clock on the nightstand—6:37 AM.

Rick was still asleep beside her, one arm slung across her waist, his breathing deep and annoyingly peaceful.

Her body was sore in all the ways she liked. Her thighs ached, her back was tight, and there was a dull throb between her legs that reminded her just how much tequila and grief had fueled last night's decisions.

But her mind?

Still empty.

Not quiet.
Just... hollow.

She slipped out from under Rick's arm as gently as she could, careful not to wake him, and padded across the cold tile floor to the bathroom. She flipped on the light and winced. Her eyeliner had migrated halfway to her cheekbone. Her lipstick was gone. Her ponytail had become a half-matted mess of hair that screamed "I just survived the emotional apocalypse."

She turned on the sink and splashed cold water on her face, staring at herself in the mirror.

This wasn't her.

This wasn't how she usually looked after a Friday night. She wasn't the kind of woman who stayed in a man's bed until morning or woke up in someone else's home like she had something to prove.

But today?

She had needed this.

Not the sex.

The silence.

The stillness.

The momentary escape from a world where kids died in tents and no one gave a shit.

She got dressed quietly, grabbed her coat off the floor, and left Rick a note on a sticky pad by the fridge:

Thanks for last night.
 No breakfast needed.
 —E

Then she called an Uber, sat in the back seat with her head leaned against the cool window, and didn't speak a word the entire ride home.

When she walked into the school office later that morning, slightly late but polished enough to pass inspection, the air hit her like a wall of too-bright fluorescence and cheap coffee.

She had barely made it three steps past the counter when Mateo popped up from behind a stack of manila folders like a glittery meerkat.

"Well, well, well," he said, sipping from his rhinestone-covered tumbler with a paper straw. "Look who finally decided to rise from the ashes of her own ho phase."

Elizabeth raised an eyebrow. "Good morning to you too, sunshine."

Mateo gave her a full once-over. "You're walking with a limp and your hair has exactly one stubborn piece doing a post-coital pirouette on the left side. So either you slipped on a banana peel this morning or Rick got a 10/10 Yelp review last night."

Elizabeth groaned. "Jesus, Mateo."

He held up a finger. "Saint Mateo, if we're being formal."

"I'm serious," she said, adjusting her blazer. "I need caffeine, a plan, and for you to stop speaking."

"Too bad," he said, walking beside her. "Because I brewed your favorite."

Elizabeth's eyes widened. "Hazelnut?"

"Hazelnut. No cinnamon sabotage. I defended the pot like a barista gladiator this morning." Mateo leaned in over his desk, looked to his left, then right and giggled, "And Linda has been on the hunt for her cinnamon all morning."

She stopped. Turned to face him. "I would take a bullet for you."

Mateo bowed slightly. "I accept your loyalty, peasant."

Elizabeth cracked a small, genuine smile for the first time all morning.

God, she needed him.

Mateo had a gift. He didn't ignore pain. He danced around it until she could breathe again.

"Seriously though," he said more gently, placing a hand on her shoulder. "You okay?"

She hesitated.

Thought about lying.

Then shrugged. "Not even close."

He nodded. "Good. That's better than pretending."

Back in her office, Elizabeth sat down with the hazelnut coffee cradled in her hands like it was a newborn. She stared at the mug. Let the steam rise up and sting her eyes.

There was still work to do.

Still a war to fight.

Still a broken system to confront.

Craig was gone. But she wasn't.

And as long as she was here?

She wasn't done.

Not by a long shot.

Eight

The morning sunlight slanted across Elizabeth's desk, cutting through the blinds in sharp, golden lines that painted the office like a crime scene. Dust motes floated lazily in the still air, suspended like secrets.

Elizabeth sat perfectly still, her fingers tapping lightly against her desk, the rhythm steady but anxious. In front of her sat a manila folder with a fresh enrollment packet for a student named Emily Carson.

The documents were filled out completely—too completely.

Flawless penmanship. No crossed-out mistakes. The kind of attention to detail that didn't feel maternal or chaotic or stressed like most enrollment packets.

It felt *deliberate*.

She flipped to the birth certificate and stared at it for the third time.

It was wrong.

She couldn't immediately explain how—there was no glaring error, no blood-red flag—but something about it screamed *off.* The font was slightly misaligned. The seal was faint, like it had been scanned and reprinted. And the signature at the bottom?

Too neat. Too perfect.

And if there was one thing Elizabeth had learned after years of being in schools—it was that *nothing involving real children was ever perfect.*

Miss Sillimar had been the one to bring it to her.

The elderly registrar stood in the corner of the office, clasping a clipboard to her chest like a shield. Her lips were pressed into a line, but her eyes were sharp behind her bifocals.

"I've been doing this a long time," she said softly. "That man… he gave me the creeps."

Elizabeth looked up, brows raised. Miss Sillimar was not a woman who rattled easily.

"He kept smiling," the registrar continued. "But it didn't reach his eyes. And the girl—Emily— wouldn't look up from her shoes. She wouldn't speak at all."

Elizabeth closed the folder slowly and slid it to the edge of her desk.

"Do me a favor," she said calmly. "Process it like normal, but don't send anything to the district yet. I want to verify a few things first."

Miss Sillimar gave a tight nod. "And if he calls back?"

Elizabeth leaned back in her chair. "Tell him everything is moving along as expected. Nothing to worry about."

Which was code for: *Don't let him know we're onto him.*

Miss Sillimar nodded again and walked out of the office without another word.

The door clicked softly shut behind her.

Elizabeth exhaled hard and reached for her phone.

She didn't even wait for the full ring.

"Smith," came the gravelly voice on the other end.

"You in the building?" she asked, already rolling the chair back from her desk.

A short pause.

"Yeah. What's going on?"

"I need you to run a name. Quietly."

Another pause. Then a grumble.

"Shit. Alright. Be there in five."

Click.

Elizabeth set the phone down, eyes fixed on the folder like it might start smoking.

She wasn't paranoid by nature. But she wasn't new to this game either.

She'd seen it before.

Kids registered by people who weren't who they claimed to be.

Custody disputes.

Kidnappings.

Trafficking.

The worst-case scenario always started small—with a bad signature, a nervous child, and a smile that didn't reach the eyes.

Her gut wasn't whispering anymore.

It was *screaming*.

Officer Smith entered the office like he always did—heavy boots, a thermal cup of coffee, and an expression that said *tell me who needs to be arrested and I'll bring the cuffs.*

He shut the door behind him, set his coffee down, and dropped into the chair across from her with a quiet grunt.

"Alright. Who are we looking at?"

Elizabeth pushed the file across the desk. "New enrollment. Girl named Emily Carson. Enrolled this morning. Something's wrong. Paperwork feels off."

Smith opened the folder and started flipping through. His brow furrowed almost immediately.

"Jesus. This birth certificate looks like it was printed with a potato."

Elizabeth smirked, but only briefly. "Miss Sillimar said the man who enrolled her was polite, charming—but... off. Gave her a weird vibe. Too polished."

"Too polished is always a red flag," Smith muttered. "You think it's a custody case?"

"Maybe. Or worse."

Smith stopped flipping.

Their eyes met.

The tone changed instantly.

They'd both seen worse.

Smith pulled his laptop from his bag, opened it, and began typing rapidly.

"What's his name?"

Elizabeth flipped back to the enrollment form. "Michael Carson. Claims to be her father."

Smith frowned as he typed. "That name's generic enough to be a sitcom character."

They sat in tense silence, the soft *click-clack* of keys filling the office.

Minutes passed.

Smith's expression shifted—focused, stern, and then… something else.

Something cold.

"Got a hit," he said.

Elizabeth leaned forward. "What is it?"

Smith tilted the screen toward her.

"'Michael Carson' has no digital footprint in this county. No home address, no employment history, no DMV records, no real estate holdings. It's like he appeared out of thin air."

Elizabeth frowned. "That's not possible. Even ghost parents show up somewhere."

"Unless they don't *want* to be found."

Smith clicked again, his eyes narrowing.

A moment later, he said something under his breath that made Elizabeth's stomach twist.

"What?" she asked, her voice tight.

Smith turned the screen again.

"I found a name attached to the same phone number he listed."

Elizabeth looked.

It wasn't Michael Carson.

It wasn't even close.

It was a man listed in a 2015 missing persons report—but not as the missing party.

As a suspect.

Suspected abduction.
Case closed due to lack of evidence.
Child never recovered.

Elizabeth's heart sank.

Her fingertips went numb.

And that quiet girl who wouldn't look up at Miss Sillimar?

Might not be Emily Carson at all.

Elizabeth shut the folder, her hands suddenly too steady.

"Smith," she said quietly. "We need to figure out who the hell just enrolled in my school."

Smith nodded slowly.

Then stood.

"I'll talk to a friend at Child Welfare. Off the record. Let's confirm this before we light a fire."

Elizabeth looked down at the fake birth certificate. At the name "Emily" printed across the top.

"We may already be sitting in smoke."

Nine

The hum of the overhead fluorescent lights buzzed quietly above Elizabeth's head, casting a sterile, pale wash across the walls of her office. Outside, the rustling sound of students changing classes echoed faintly through the glass panels in her door—backpacks thumping, sneakers squeaking, snippets of teenage laughter rising and fading like waves.

But in her office, everything was still.

Elizabeth sat forward, elbows on her desk, her eyes locked on the screen of Officer Smith's laptop. His thick fingers tapped slowly across the keyboard, the screen casting a cold blue glow over his furrowed brow. He didn't speak. Not yet.

The deeper his frown became, the more Elizabeth felt her chest tightening.

"You got anything?" she asked, the tension curling around her words.

Smith let out a sharp breath, leaned back in his chair, and scrubbed a hand across his bald head before rubbing his temple with a thumb. His office radio crackled softly on his shoulder, but he didn't reach for it.

"Carson's ID and birth certificate are from Maine," he said. "Everything in our systems is state-based. I can dig through California records all day, but I've hit a wall on anything out of state."

Elizabeth sat back, her fingers clenched into fists in her lap. "So what, we hit a dead end?"

Smith grimaced, his chair creaking under his weight as he shifted.

"Not completely," he said. "I'll put in a formal request through the inter-agency portal, but you know how it goes. Could be days. Could be weeks. Depends on how cooperative Maine's Department of Vital Records feels this month."

Elizabeth turned her face away for a moment, jaw tightening. Outside her window, a tree leaned into the wind, the orange leaves clinging desperately to its limbs. A gust blew them sideways like a sigh from the universe.

Red tape.

Fucking red tape.

A child could be in danger, and they were stuck waiting for someone in another state to check a box on a form.

She exhaled slowly through her nose, focusing her thoughts like a scalpel.

"Put in the request," she said. Her voice was ice. "And the second you hear anything—call me."

Smith nodded solemnly, then hesitated.

"In the meantime… what's your play?"

Elizabeth's fingers drummed against the desk—her tell when her brain was on fire. Her gaze turned inward, razor-sharp.

"Emily doesn't speak when he's around," she said, her voice low. "I'm going to ask Ashley to start checking in with her. Build something. Trust. Familiarity. If this girl needs help, she's not going to blurt it out in a conference room."

Smith leaned forward, arms resting on his knees.

"Just be careful," he said. "If that guy's dangerous and he gets spooked—he could run. Or worse."

Elizabeth's stomach twisted.

She knew.

She fucking knew.

And that's what terrified her.

The soft buzz of the desktop diffuser hummed in the background, releasing faint puffs of lavender into the air. Ashley had dimmed the overhead lights, letting warm sunlight spill in through the blinds. It gave the room a sense of peace.

Emily sat stiffly in the chair across from her, her small frame curled inward like a question mark. Her wrists, wrapped in those ever-present bands of colorful letters, rested on her lap like she was trying to hide them.

Ashley smiled gently, pen resting in her hand, not moving yet.

"So, Emily," she began, voice easy and light. "What was your old school like?"

Emily's lips parted like she might answer.

But then—there was a knock at the door.

Ashley didn't have to guess.

The door opened before she could say a word, and Michael Carson stepped inside like he owned the place.

Dressed neatly—gray sweater, clean jeans, polished loafers. His hair was styled just enough to look effortless, and his cologne followed him into the room, subtle but calculated. He smiled, teeth white and perfect.

Ashley kept her expression smooth. But inside?

Her gut screamed.

Michael slid into the seat beside Emily, uninvited, folding his hands on his knee like he belonged there.

"I hope I'm not interrupting," he said pleasantly.

"You're fine," Ashley said with a practiced smile. "We were just getting a feel for her course placement."

Emily had withdrawn again, her shoulders tight, eyes glued to a spot on the carpet. She didn't so much as blink in her direction.

Ashley pivoted.

"We're still waiting on transcripts," she said smoothly. "So I thought I'd ask about her classes in Maine. Try to match her to the right ones here."

Michael smiled, eager. "Of course. Let's see— she had Algebra with Mr. Turner. English Lit with Ms. Benson. Biology with Mr. Thomas. Coach Hall ran her P.E."

Ashley nodded, writing it all down, cataloging each detail. The speed of his answers was off. Too perfect. Too ready.

"And what school was that again?"

"Rockland High School," Michael replied instantly, too smoothly.

Too prepared.

Emily remained silent, hands pressed so tightly into her lap that her fingers turned white.

Elizabeth watched her, not Michael. If Emily had any reaction to the name of her supposed school, it wasn't visible. No nod, no flicker of recognition.

That was wrong.

Kids always had some reaction when you named their old school—nostalgia, boredom, even mild irritation. But nothing? That was unnatural.

She made a mental note: Verify school before day's end.

Ashley felt her skin crawl.

She leaned back casually. "That's great. I'll go ahead and request the records directly from Rockland to confirm."

Michael's eyes flicked up.

Only for a second.

But it was enough.

"I actually have them at home," he said quickly. "I'll bring them tomorrow."

Ashley smiled politely, hiding the dagger behind her teeth.

"We'll still need to confirm them through official channels," she said with an easy nod. "Just standard procedure."

Michael's smile flickered.

But only for a moment.

"Of course."

Ashley stood. "I'll walk you out."

The afternoon breeze tugged at Ashley's cardigan as they stepped through the front doors. Leaves swirled along the pavement, the air crisp and clean, the sky a watercolor of soft clouds.

Michael lit a cigarette at the curb.

"I think I'll take a minute," he said. "Long day."

Ashley's eyes slid over him, calm and curious. But inside, her brain was racing.

He wasn't walking to a car.

Wasn't reaching for keys.

He knew she wanted the plate.

And he wasn't going to let her get it.

She smiled sweetly. "Enjoy your smoke."

And turned back inside.

Tiffany's workspace was clinical but cozy— stacked files, a soft lamp, and the faint scent of eucalyptus hand lotion.

Ashley dropped into the chair across from her, exhausted.

"Emily Carson," she said flatly.

Tiffany raised an eyebrow. "I've been waiting for you."

Ashley sighed. "We need to verify everything. Immunizations. Vitals. Height, weight, vision, dental. If there's something off, it might be in her file."

Tiffany nodded. "You think this is an identity issue?"

"I think," Ashley said slowly, "this girl is a ghost. And he's not her dad."

Tiffany didn't blink. "I'll call her in tomorrow."

Ashley stood.

"Thank you," she said. "And if you see anything—anything weird—call me first. Before you call anyone else."

Tiffany nodded solemnly. "I've got your back."

Elizabeth sat in her car in the driveway, the sky darkening around her, headlights from a neighbor's car briefly illuminating the inside of her vehicle.

She hadn't turned off the engine.

Her phone buzzed in the passenger seat.

Rick: Hey. Dinner still on?

Elizabeth stared at it.

She needed the break.

She needed to breathe.

ELIZABETH: Still on. 7.

The restaurant was dim and cozy, tucked inside a quiet street in the historic district. String lights glowed above their patio table, and a votive candle flickered between her and Rick, casting soft shadows on their faces.

Rick smiled as she slid into her chair, slightly breathless from being ten minutes late. He wore a crisp shirt, sleeves rolled just enough to hint at the relaxed confidence he always seemed to carry.

"You made it," he said.

"Barely," she replied, managing a smile.

Rick nodded toward the wine list. "You want your usual?"

Elizabeth didn't hesitate. "Glass of Pinot Noir, please."

Rick lifted an eyebrow knowingly but didn't comment. He signaled the waiter.

They ordered, but Elizabeth barely touched the food. Her mind was still caught in the static of red flags and false records and a quiet girl who might be someone else entirely. Rick tried to keep the conversation light, and she appreciated that, even if she didn't really respond much.

"It's really nice being here with you," she said finally. "I don't have to solve anything. I can just... be."

Rick smiled, his hand brushing gently over hers.

The warmth of his touch grounded her, just enough to make her forget—for a minute.

The night air was crisp as they walked to Rick's car, hands brushing together, laughter slipping a little easier now. By the time they reached his place, the tension in Elizabeth's shoulders had eased just enough for her to stop overthinking.

Inside, she dropped her heels by the door, shrugging off her coat. Rick turned to face her, and in the dim kitchen light, she looked up and whispered, "I don't want to talk anymore."

His mouth met hers before the sentence even finished.

He lifted her easily, carrying her down the hall, her legs wrapped around him, her breath hot on his neck.

Their clothes left a trail across the hardwood floor—her blouse, his belt, her skirt, his shirt. Every kiss grew hungrier, every touch more urgent. In his bedroom, she took control, guiding him to the bed, climbing over him like a woman who finally allowed herself to feel.

Elizabeth rode the edge of pleasure and control, gripping his wrists, whispering filth into his ear. She kissed the base of his throat, sucked along his jawline, and gasped when he rolled them, taking control. Her body arched under him, and she moaned as he hit the perfect rhythm—just hard enough, just deep enough, no need for gentle.

It was exactly what she wanted.

Needed.

Until he said it.

"I love you," Rick whispered, just above a breath, as he thrust into her.

Elizabeth froze.

Her body tensed mid-movement. Her hand, which had been tangled in his hair, went still.

What the fuck did he just say?

Her mind screamed. She wanted to disappear. Not now. Not in the middle of this. Not when everything else in her life was already on fire.

Maybe if I pretend I didn't hear it, he won't say it again.

Rick kissed her collarbone, oblivious, wrapping his arms tightly around her as they both collapsed into the sheets.

Elizabeth lay on her back, staring at the ceiling like it was a blank screen. Her eyes didn't blink. Her thoughts didn't stop.

Rick nuzzled into her, whispering something soft and sweet, his fingers tracing light patterns across her skin. He pulled her close like she was something delicate.

She wasn't.

She didn't want to be.

He held her like a teddy bear.

And she stared at the wall, eyes wide open.

Brick by brick, the wall inside her rebuilt itself.

Emotionally detached.

Mentally somewhere else.

She was gone again.

Because love wasn't what she needed. Not right now. Not when a child might be living a lie, hiding in plain sight, waiting for someone to notice she didn't belong.

Elizabeth lay there, quiet—confused and somewhat scared.

But she began planning her next move.

Ten

The mid-morning sun filtered through the slats of Elizabeth's office blinds, casting striped shadows across her desk. Dust motes floated lazily in the beam of light, dancing through the still air. Outside, the low murmur of student chatter filled the quad—distant, like background noise in a world she wasn't a part of today.

Elizabeth leaned back against the edge of her desk, one arm folded tightly across her stomach, the other tapping a pen against a neon yellow sticky note. Scrawled across it in sharp, slanted handwriting was a license plate number.

She stared at it like it owed her answers.

Her phone rang.

She answered before the first full ring.

"Smith, tell me you found something," she said, her voice clipped, sharp.

On the other end, Officer Smith let out a long sigh, the kind of sound that made her stomach drop.

"We ran the plates," he said. "The vehicle is registered to a rental address. Doesn't match what Carson listed on Emily's paperwork."

Elizabeth closed her eyes for a beat, exhaling through her nose.

"How far off?" she asked.

"Across town," Smith said. "East side. Property's under a short-term lease, no long-term tenancy. And get this—Michael Carson's name isn't attached to any property in California. Nothing. No rental agreements, no utility bills, no property taxes. He's a ghost."

Elizabeth felt her jaw clench. Her molars ground together like gears.

"So, he lied about where they live."

"Looks that way," Smith confirmed. "Either he's incredibly good at covering his tracks, or he's not who he says he is. Hell, maybe both."

Elizabeth stood up and paced the office, the heel of her shoe clicking against the tile like a metronome of fury.

"Can you request more from Maine? Birth records, past addresses, criminal history, anything?"

"Already in motion," Smith said. "But it's slow. You know how it is—multiple agencies, outdated systems, someone on vacation—takes one person to stall the whole thing."

"Goddamn red tape," Elizabeth muttered.

"Yep," Smith replied. "Time's the biggest problem right now."

Elizabeth stopped pacing, her hand braced on the edge of the window. She stared outside, watching a group of students laughing by the vending machine.

Time.

That's what she didn't have.

Not if Emily was in danger.

She hung up, then immediately dialed Ashley.

Ashley answered on the second ring. Her voice was tight, like she already knew what Elizabeth was going to say.

"Tell me you've got something."

Elizabeth didn't waste breath. "Michael Carson's address is fake. His car's registered to a short-term rental, and his name doesn't show up anywhere in the state. Not on paper, not online, not even in DMV records."

Ashley sighed. "So the guy who walks and talks like a cardboard cutout just confirmed he's hiding something."

"Exactly. Still no school records. He says he'll bring them. I don't trust it."

"I wouldn't either," Ashley said. "I've set up a meeting with Emily today. Just her. No Michael."

Elizabeth felt a flicker of relief cut through the stress like a clean inhale.

"Good," she said. "We need to know who she is. What her story is. And we need it before he decides to pull her and vanish."

Ashley paused for a beat. "I've done this before, Liz. But this one?"

Elizabeth nodded slowly. "This one feels different."

There was silence on the line before Ashley answered.

"It is."

The diffuser in the corner released a slow curl of vanilla mist. Ashley had turned off the fluorescent lights and opened the blinds just enough to let the daylight soften the room's edges.

Emily Carson sat in the same chair she always did—small frame folded inward, arms wrapped loosely across her stomach, her gaze never quite meeting Ashley's. Her wrists were still wrapped in those strange lettered bracelets, her fingers twitching like they wanted to fidget but didn't dare.

Ashley gave her a warm, practiced smile.

"You getting used to the campus a little bit?"

Emily nodded, barely.

Ashley leaned back slightly, voice soft. "Any teachers standing out so far? Mr. Garza for math? He's got the worst dad jokes, but he's a legend."

A second nod.

Still no words.

Ashley didn't push. Not yet.

She studied the girl's posture—rigid spine, chin low, knuckles white against her sleeves.

"You said you liked math. What else? Did you do sports back in Maine?"

Emily blinked slowly. Her lips parted just slightly. She shifted in her seat.

Ashley leaned forward just an inch, heart catching in her throat.

But then—
A knock at the door.

Ashley's heart sank like an anchor.

The door opened, and there he was.

Michael Carson.

He stepped in with the same easy calm he always wore like a tailored suit. Polished loafers. No wrinkles in his shirt. Perfect smile. But his eyes? His eyes were always scanning, calculating, storing.

"I hope I'm not interrupting," he said with a smooth smile.

Ashley turned that same smile back on him, ice beneath the sugar.

"Of course not," she lied. "We were just talking about classes. Getting a feel for where Emily fits."

Michael walked in and sat without asking. Emily folded in on herself like a house collapsing inward.

Ashley watched it all—Emily's silence, her shrinking. Michael's control. The show.

"She had Turner for Algebra, Benson for English, and Coach Hall for P.E.," Michael said easily. "Rockland High School. She was there two years."

Ashley's pen didn't stop moving.

"And you'll be bringing her transcripts?"

"I have them at home," Michael said, just a touch too quickly. "I'll bring them tomorrow."

Ashley smiled politely.

"That's great. But we'll still request official records from the district office, just to verify everything for our system."

It was slight—but she saw it.

His jaw clenched.

And his fingers twitched once.

He didn't like that.

Not at all.

Tiffany was logging new medical forms when Ashley walked in. The sharp scent of antiseptic floated faintly beneath her floral perfume.

Ashley shut the door softly behind her.

"Emily Carson," she said.

Tiffany didn't look surprised.

"I thought so," she said. "You want me to call her in?"

Ashley nodded. "Vision screen. Vitals. Check her immunization records. If she's not who she says she is, it might show up somewhere in there."

Tiffany's eyes narrowed with focus. "You think this guy kidnapped her?"

"I don't know," Ashley said, voice tight. "But he's hiding something. And she's terrified of him."

Tiffany stood. "I'll pull her tomorrow morning. We'll see what turns up."

Ashley exhaled slowly.

And as she walked out of the room, one thought repeated over and over in her head:

They were getting close.
 And Michael Carson could feel it

Eleven

Elizabeth pulled up to the curb, putting her car in park as she stared at the old brick building. It stood on a downtown street corner, wedged between a rundown laundromat with flickering fluorescent lights and a liquor store that advertised COLD BEER & EBT ACCEPTED in peeling vinyl letters. The streets were mostly empty this late in the evening, save for a few stragglers—an older man pushing a shopping cart filled with cans, a group of teenagers loitering outside a vape shop, and a lone cyclist pedaling through the dim glow of the streetlights.

The KICKBOXING | SELF-DEFENSE | MMA sign above the entrance was faded, its once-bold red letters now chipped and weathered. The front door was propped open, letting out the deep bass of music and the rhythmic thuds of fists hitting pads. The interior lighting cast a hazy yellow glow through the tinted windows, but Elizabeth still couldn't see much inside.

She clenched the steering wheel for a beat before taking a slow breath. This is it. She had spent too many sleepless nights thinking about this—about doing something, about taking control. The system had failed Craig. She refused to be powerless again.

With that thought, she stepped out of the car.

Inside, the gym smelled like sweat, leather, and determination. The air was thick with it, mingling with the distinct scent of disinfectant and old vinyl mats. The space was utilitarian— no fancy equipment, no plush yoga mats, just heavy bags lined against the exposed brick walls, scuffed-up floors, and motivational posters screaming at her:

TRAIN HARD OR GO HOME.
PAIN IS WEAKNESS LEAVING THE BODY.
FIGHT LIKE YOU MEAN IT.

Her eyes flicked over the people stretching on the mats. A mix of middle-aged men reliving their glory days, exhausted new moms eager to reclaim their pre-baby strength, and a few gym rats who probably did this as a warm-up before lifting. The instructor—a lean, sharp-eyed man with tattooed arms—stood near the front, wrapping his hands with the casual confidence of someone who knew exactly what he was capable of.

Elizabeth signed the waiver at the front desk, barely acknowledged by a bored teenager scrolling on his phone. She grabbed a pair of loaner wraps and moved to an open space on the mat, scanning the room as she wound the fabric around her knuckles. This is fine, she told herself. I'll start with this. I need the conditioning, anyway.

Except… the moment the warm-up began, she knew it wasn't enough.

The movements were familiar. Jab, cross, hook. She had thrown these punches before, had even been pretty good at them back in college when she went through her brief "fitness phase." But now? This felt like shadowboxing. A cardio routine disguised as combat.

She needed more. More than just sweating and burning calories. More than just learning how to hit a bag that wouldn't hit back. She needed something real. Something brutal.

She caught the instructor—Simon, according to the patch on his shorts—watching her between combinations. His eyes flicked from her stance to her strikes, then past her, toward the farthest corner of the gym. Reading her.

The workout ended too soon, leaving her chest heaving with frustration more than exertion. She hadn't come here to feel better. She had come here to get stronger.

As she unwrapped her hands, Simon approached, a towel slung over his shoulder.

"You're fit," he said, nodding toward her. "Strong. But you're not here for kickboxing."

Elizabeth lifted a brow. "No?"

Simon smirked, as if he had been waiting for her to ask. "Nah. You want something more than a workout."

She let out a breath. "What do you suggest?"

He jerked his head toward the darkened corner of the gym, where a separate training area sat behind a black partition. The space was dimly lit, nearly empty, except for one figure—a man, old and wiry, his back to them as he worked a heavy bag with slow, deliberate strikes. His punches were nothing flashy. Nothing dramatic. Just efficient. Deadly.

"You should check out the Krav Maga sessions," Simon said. "That's what you're really looking for."

Elizabeth squinted toward the old man. His build was compact but coiled tight with sinewy strength. His clothes were loose but functional—just a plain black T-shirt and faded training pants. But his movements? They were precise, controlled, the kind of controlled that meant he could break someone in half if he wanted to.

"Who's the instructor?" she asked.

Simon's lips twitched. "Abraham."

Elizabeth exhaled sharply and muttered under her breath, "Jesus—is that Splinter?"

She hadn't meant to say it loud enough for Simon to hear, but his sharp chuckle told her otherwise.

Elizabeth flushed, more from embarrassment than the grueling workout.

Simon just grinned. "Go talk to him. If you're serious about learning, he'll know."

She hesitated for only a second before heading toward the back room.

The air in the training room was different. Heavy. No mirrors, no music. Just a few worn mats and the quiet, steady sound of fists meeting vinyl.

Abraham didn't look up when she approached. His hands, wrapped in old cloth instead of gloves, moved with unshakable precision— each strike against the heavy bag landing with a controlled, brutal rhythm.

Elizabeth stopped a few feet away, waiting. He didn't acknowledge her.

Finally, she cleared her throat. "Simon told me to come talk to you."

Silence.

Then, without looking, Abraham tossed a pair of gloves at her feet.

She hesitated for only a second before bending to pick them up.

She slid them on, tightening the straps, watching as he finally turned to face her. His face was lined, weathered, eyes sharp beneath thick, graying brows. His knuckles were scarred, hands like old leather from a lifetime of fights.

But there was something deeper there. Something dark. A story not yet told.

Without a word, he lifted his hands, signaling for her to begin.

Elizabeth threw a punch.

It was good. Controlled. But not enough.

She threw another.

Harder.

With every strike, something inside her uncoiled. The frustration. The helplessness.

The grief she had swallowed whole. It poured into every movement, every impact.

Abraham watched her without expression, absorbing every ounce of her fury, every bit of the weight she carried.

Then, finally, he spoke.

"You're here because the law failed you."

Elizabeth froze. Her next punch landed weaker than the last. Her eyes snapped to his, searching.

"How did you know?" she asked, breathless.

Abraham didn't answer right away. Instead, he unwrapped his sleeve, rolling it up to reveal a long, ugly scar that ran from wrist to elbow. The skin was gnarled, twisted, a painful story woven into his flesh.

"They failed me, too," he said simply.

Elizabeth's fists tightened inside her gloves.

She didn't ask what happened to him.

She already knew.

And for the first time in a long time, she felt understood.

Twelve

Ashley nearly dropped her wine glass.

"You're doing what?"

Elizabeth leaned back on the patio couch, stretching her sore legs out in front of her. The night air was crisp, carrying the scent of distant barbecue smoke and freshly cut grass. A half-empty bottle of Pinot Noir sat on the table between them, Elizabeth absently swirling the deep red liquid in her glass. Every muscle in her body throbbed from training. Her shoulders ached, her knuckles still burned from earlier drills, and the faint bruises along her forearms were darkening by the second.

Worth it.

"Krav Maga," she repeated, taking a slow sip. "With an old war dog named Abraham."

Ashley's eyebrows shot up. "And why, exactly, do you need to know how to disarm a man twice your size?"

Elizabeth smirked. "I don't need to. I want to."

Ashley gave her a long, measured look. She knew Elizabeth better than most people. And right now? Elizabeth was lying. Or at least, not telling the whole truth.

"You okay?" Ashley asked, softer this time.

Elizabeth exhaled, her gaze drifting toward the darkened yard. A single porch light cast long shadows across the patio, illuminating the condensation on their wine glasses but not quite reaching the edge of the fence. Beyond that was darkness. And for the first time in her life, Elizabeth was beginning to realize she didn't mind the dark.

She took another slow sip before answering.

"Not really," she admitted. "But this helps."

Ashley didn't press. She knew better. She knew when Elizabeth wasn't ready to talk. But from that moment on, she made a silent vow—if Elizabeth was going to walk into darkness, she wouldn't let her go alone.

Across the patio table, Elizabeth's phone lit up.

A message from Rick.

RICK: *Hey. We should talk.*

Her stomach twisted. She ignored it, flipping the phone face-down like it might stop the thoughts from creeping in.

Ashley, however, noticed everything. Of course, she did.

Her eyes flicked toward the phone, then back to Elizabeth. "Rick?"

Elizabeth swirled her wine. "Yeah."

Ashley took another sip, waiting for more. When Elizabeth stayed silent, she sighed. "You haven't answered him, have you?"

Elizabeth exhaled through her nose. "Nope."

Ashley shook her head but didn't push. Elizabeth wasn't ready for that conversation. And honestly? Maybe she never would be.

Mateo was getting suspicious.

Elizabeth had always been a little intense, but lately, something was different.

She was moving slower, wincing when she thought no one was looking. Her usually flawless posture had developed a stiffness, like her body had been through hell but she refused to let anyone see it.

One morning, when she reached for a stack of paperwork, he caught sight of the bruises.

Dark, angry rings wrapping around her wrist like handcuffs.

He narrowed his eyes. "Alright," he said, crossing his arms. "Either you're fighting crime at night or you've taken up medieval jousting. Spill."

Elizabeth didn't even look up from her desk. "Drop it, Mateo."

"Yeah, see, that response only makes me want to push harder."

She sighed, pressing her fingers to her temples. "I picked up a hobby. That's all."

Mateo leaned against the doorframe, unconvinced. "Uh-huh. And does this 'hobby' involve hand-to-hand combat with a grumpy seventy-year-old man?"

Elizabeth finally glanced at him, and for a split second, he saw something flicker behind her eyes.

A challenge. A warning.

"Drop it," she repeated, slower this time.

Mateo didn't.

He just started watching her more closely.

"You need stitches."

Elizabeth winced as Tiffany pressed a disinfectant wipe against her shoulder.

She sat on the nurse's office cot, her blazer discarded on the chair beside her, the white tank top she wore beneath it speckled with blood from a cut just above her collarbone.

"I don't have time," Elizabeth muttered.

Tiffany arched a brow. "You will if your shoulder gets infected."

Elizabeth groaned but didn't argue. She never did with Tiffany.

The woman had an almost unnerving ability to read bullshit a mile away. Tiffany pulled out a sterile needle and thread, setting up for a quick suture.

"You should probably be asking me what happened," Elizabeth said dryly.

Tiffany didn't even look up as she threaded the needle. "I should. But we both know you're not going to tell me."

Elizabeth smirked. "Smart woman."

Tiffany's eyes flicked up, pinning her with a look that was equal parts amusement and exasperation. "Damn right I am."

As Tiffany worked, Elizabeth's phone buzzed again on the counter.

RICK: *Just tell me where we stand.*

Elizabeth clenched her jaw but didn't reach for it.

Tiffany raised an eyebrow but said nothing. She just tied the last suture and patted Elizabeth's shoulder, not unkindly.

She never asked questions. She just patched her up.

Elizabeth sat in her office later that evening, door locked, fingers tapping lightly against the armrest of her chair.

Her phone buzzed again.

RICK: *Liz, please. Just talk to me.*

Her stomach twisted, just like it had the first time he said it.

I love you.

She had never wanted to hear those words. Not from him. Not from anyone.

The problem wasn't Rick. He was a good man. Kind. Reliable. Safe.

The problem was her.

She had spent her entire career building walls. Standing between kids and the chaos of their lives. And now? She had walked willingly into the shadows.

How was she supposed to let someone in when she had no intention of ever coming back?

The phone buzzed again.

She let it ring.

Then, without hesitation, she turned it off.

She had more important things to deal with.

Elizabeth had spent years fighting for kids within the system.

But now?

She was starting to think the real fight was outside of it.

And she was ready.

Even if it meant losing herself completely.

It was her administrative decision.

Thirteen

Ashley sat across from Emily, keeping her posture relaxed, her voice light, her demeanor open. No pressure. No sudden movements. Just patience.

The office was quiet except for the hum of the old air conditioning unit in the corner. The blinds were slightly open, letting in slats of dull afternoon light that barely touched the worn-out rug beneath their chairs. Emily sat stiffly, hands clasped together in her lap, fingers nervously twisting the frayed edges of her hoodie sleeves.

But today?

She wasn't completely shut down.

Ashley took a slow sip from her coffee mug, setting it down carefully before meeting Emily's gaze.

"Emily," she said gently. "Is Michael really your dad?"

The room went still.

Emily's breath hitched, and her fingers tightened around her sleeve. Her gaze dropped to the floor, her lips pressing into a thin, uncertain line.

Ashley didn't move, didn't press. She just waited.

And then, so quietly it was almost lost under the hum of the AC, Emily whispered—

"No."

Ashley's heart clenched.

Emily inhaled sharply, blinking fast, like she was trying to stop herself from crying.

"He says I'm supposed to be Emily now."

Ashley's throat went dry. Now. As if she hadn't always been Emily.

Ashley's stomach twisted into a knot. She leaned in slightly, keeping her voice calm, steady.

"What about your mom?"

Emily swallowed hard. Her hands balled into fists.

"She's gone."

Ashley's heart pounded against her ribs.

Emily's voice cracked. "I le won't say why."

A single tear slipped down Emily's cheek, but she didn't wipe it away.

Ashley felt the weight of the moment settle into her bones.

This was it. The moment she knew Elizabeth had been right all along. The moment that would change everything.

Emily took a shaky breath, her voice barely above a whisper.

"There's a camera in the house."

Ashley stilled.

Emily's hands trembled slightly in her lap as she kept her eyes trained downward.

"It's locked in a safe."

Ashley's pulse spiked.

This was it. Proof.

She pulled her phone from her pocket under the desk, fingers moving fast.

Ashley: We have a problem. We need to talk. Now.

The reply was instant.

Elizabeth: What happened?

Ashley: Emily just told me there's a camera in the house. Locked in a safe.

Elizabeth: That's it. We're getting that camera.

Ashley took a deep breath, forcing herself to stay steady for Emily.

"Emily," she said gently. "Can you tell me anything else?"

Emily hesitated, then shook her head quickly.

"He'll know I talked," she whispered. "If I say more, he'll know."

Ashley felt a chill creep down her spine.

Michael was controlling her. He had made sure she lived in fear of what he might do.

But it wasn't just control.

It was something much worse.

Ashley knew, deep in her gut, that Michael had hurt people before.

And Emily's mother?

She might already be dead.

Elizabeth stormed into Officer Smith's office minutes later.

"Tell me you found something," she demanded, slamming the door behind her.

Smith, seated at his desk, leaned back with a sigh, rubbing his temple.

"We ran him again." His voice was gruff, grim. "Michael Carson is not Emily's father. He married Sarah Keller two years ago, when Emily was ten."

Elizabeth's fingernails dug into her palms.

"Where's Sarah?" she asked.

Smith exhaled heavily. "That's the problem. Sarah Keller disappeared in Maine under mysterious circumstances."

Elizabeth's jaw tightened.

"What kind of 'mysterious'?" she demanded.

Smith's expression darkened. "Reported missing by her sister over a year ago. Police opened a case, but there was no evidence of foul play—at least none they could prove. Then, about six weeks after she vanished, Michael left Maine. Took Emily with him."

Elizabeth felt a fire ignite in her chest.

"So he snatched Emily," she said, voice flat.

Smith nodded. "Looks that way."

Elizabeth clenched her fists.

"This guy's dangerous."

Smith met her gaze.

"No doubt about it."

Elizabeth's mind raced.

The safe.

That camera.

That was their only shot at proof.

And if the system wasn't going to help?

She'd get it herself.

The gym smelled like blood, old sweat, and rubber flooring. The overhead light flickered faintly above Elizabeth as she stood in the back corner of the training room, heart still pounding from the earlier drills. Her body was bruised and aching, her shoulder taped from last week's sparring session, but tonight she hadn't come for hand-to-hand.

She'd come for something else.

Abraham stood at the heavy bag, his back to her, delivering slow, precise strikes. His breathing was steady. Controlled. He hadn't said a word since she entered. He never spoke first. That was part of his training: if you needed something, you asked.

Elizabeth exhaled through her nose. "I need to learn how to crack a safe."

Abraham didn't stop punching.

"You planning to rob a bank?"

She gave a humorless smirk. "Not unless the bank's storing proof a child is being abused."

Now he paused. Just for a moment. Then he turned, eyes sharp beneath those thick brows.

"What kind of safe?"

"Small. Home model. Combination dial. Probably bolted to the floor."

Abraham nodded once, then walked past her without another word. He disappeared into the back storage room. Elizabeth followed.

Inside, the air was cooler, filled with the scent of metal polish and old gear. Abraham flipped on a light, then pulled a beat-up practice safe from beneath a shelf. It was scarred with dents, worn around the dial from years of use.

"We use this for conditioning," he said. "Teaches patience. Precision."

He dropped it onto the metal table with a loud clang, then motioned for her to sit.

"The dial's your enemy and your friend. Feel for the tension. Don't fight it. Read it."

She sat. Her fingers hovered over the dial.

"It's not about speed," he continued. "It's about control. Just like fighting. You force it, you lose."

Elizabeth placed her hand on the dial. Closed her eyes. Began to turn.

Hours passed. Maybe minutes. She lost track. The world narrowed to the subtle clicks beneath her fingertips, the quiet breath between numbers. Abraham didn't speak again. He didn't need to. His presence anchored her.

And finally—

Click.

The lock gave. The dial stopped. The safe door creaked open.

Elizabeth stared at it, chest tight. It was just training. Just practice. But it felt like more.

Abraham nodded slowly. "You're ready."

She stood, wiping sweat from her brow. Her hands trembled, but her spine was straight.

"Thank you," she said.

Abraham stepped back, folding his arms. "Don't use it for the wrong reasons."

Elizabeth's jaw tightened. "I won't."

She left without another word.

In two days, she would use what he taught her. And this time, it wouldn't be a drill.

Fourteen

The midnight rain came down in sheets, hammering against rooftops and flooding the gutters. The streetlights flickered, struggling against the storm, casting long, uneven shadows across the neighborhood.

Elizabeth crouched behind a row of overgrown bushes, her breath slow and measured. She was ready.

Dressed in all black, her fitted thermal clinging to her rain-dampened skin, her combat boots planted firmly in the mud, she was more than just Elizabeth Kane, Assistant Principal. She was something else tonight.

The black streaks of face paint across her skin blended her into the night. The storm had knocked out the power—no cameras, no alarms.

Perfect.

She had studied Michael Carson's routine. He should still be out.

A gust of wind sent the porch swing creaking, the sound nearly swallowed by the downpour.

Elizabeth's fingers curled around the cold metal of the fence as she hoisted herself over, landing silently in the backyard.

A shutter banged against the house, and for a split second, she thought the noise was something else—someone waiting. Watching.

But the house remained still.

Elizabeth swallowed, steadying her breath, and moved toward the window she had scouted days before. Unlocked. Just like she'd hoped.

She slipped inside.

The air inside the house was thick with humidity. The scent of old wood, stale cologne, and something faintly metallic hung in the air.

The floorboards beneath her boots were uneven, warped from years of neglect. Each step was calculated, silent.

She didn't have much time.

Elizabeth had memorized the layout. The safe was in the master bedroom closet—tucked beneath a row of stacked boxes and a pile of discarded coats.

She moved carefully through the hallway, pausing to listen.

Nothing.

The wind howled through the cracks of the old house, and the storm rattled against the glass, masking any noise she might make.

She reached the bedroom and slipped inside, shutting the door just enough to keep it from creaking.

The closet was just as she'd expected— cluttered, chaotic, but hiding exactly what she was looking for.

Her fingers brushed against cold steel.

Found it.

The safe was heavy, bolted down. Combination lock. Standard. But she had studied Michael for weeks. She had watched the way his fingers moved when he spun the lock—casual, but deliberate. He was repetitive in his actions.

And Elizabeth was very, very good at paying attention.

She turned the dial slowly, testing the resistance.

First number. Click.

Her breath stayed even.

Second number. Click.

Almost there.

Third—

A floorboard groaned.

Elizabeth's heart stopped.

She wasn't alone.

A low exhale.

The sound of heavy boots shifting.

Elizabeth froze.

Michael.

He shouldn't have been home.

The safe no longer mattered. She had to get out.

She turned, moving toward the door—

Too late.

The darkness exploded into motion.

Michael lunged from the shadows, swinging hard.

Elizabeth ducked, but not fast enough.

His fist slammed into her shoulder, sending her staggering into the closet door. Pain shot through her ribs, but she recovered fast, twisting away before his second strike could connect.

Breathe. Focus. React.

Abraham's voice echoed in her head.

Elizabeth snapped her arm up, blocking his next attack, then struck hard and fast—a palm to the chin, a knee to the ribs.

Michael grunted, stumbling back.

She tried to push past him, but he recovered too quickly.

A flicker of silver—

Knife.

Elizabeth jerked back just as the blade sliced across her shoulder.

White-hot pain tore through her.

She gasped but didn't let herself freeze.

Instead, she drove her elbow into his sternum. Hard.

Michael cursed, staggering.

That was her chance.

Elizabeth bolted, ignoring the burn in her shoulder, ignoring the pain shooting down her arm.

She sprinted down the hall, past the kitchen, through the back door—

Rain slammed against her skin, the cold shocking her senses.

She didn't stop. Didn't look back.

She vaulted over the fence, landing hard on the wet pavement.

Her body screamed in protest, but she forced herself to keep running.

Only when she reached her car—several blocks away, safely out of sight—did she finally stop.

Her hands trembled. Her shoulder throbbed. Blood soaked into her sleeve.

She pressed her forehead against the steering wheel.

Too close.

Way too close.

She had to be smarter.

This wasn't over.

Elizabeth walked into school limping.

The halls were already buzzing with students, but she barely heard them. Her body ached, her shoulder burned, but she kept her expression neutral. Controlled.

She wouldn't let anyone see her weak.

She reached the main office, forcing herself to stand tall.

Mateo glanced up from the front desk—and immediately narrowed his eyes.

"Okay, seriously," he said, eyeing her stiff posture. "Who are you fighting at night? Batman?"

Elizabeth forced a dry smirk.

"Dropped a shelf on myself," she lied smoothly, grabbing a folder from his desk.

Mateo didn't buy it. Not even for a second.

Before he could push, the door opened.

Elizabeth turned—

And locked eyes with Michael Carson.

For a split second, neither of them moved.

Then, Michael's gaze dropped.

Straight to the bandage peeking out from beneath her blouse.

Realization flashed in his eyes.

Recognition.

Elizabeth didn't blink. Didn't look away.

But she knew.

So did he.

He knew.

And now?

This was war.

Fifteen

Elizabeth had barely settled into her office when her phone buzzed.

SCHWARTZ: *My office. Now.*

No greeting. No pleasantries. Just a summons.

Her gut twisted. Was this about Michael Carson? Had he gone to Schwartz with some fabricated complaint? Was this about her bruises, her limp, the whisper of suspicion that was starting to spread through the school?

With a slow exhale, she pushed to her feet, rolling the tension from her shoulders as she crossed the hallway to Schwartz's office. The door was ajar, the familiar scent of coffee and worn leather greeting her as she stepped inside.

Schwartz sat behind his desk, leaning back in his chair. His expression was unreadable—serious, but not angry. Not disappointed.

That was good.

"Close the door," he said.

Elizabeth did.

Then, without preamble—

"I'm retiring," Schwartz said. "Next year."

Elizabeth froze.

For a moment, the words didn't make sense. Like her brain was trying to rearrange them into something different, something less shocking.

Retiring?

No. No, that wasn't right. Schwartz had been here forever. He was the backbone of this school, the anchor, the leader she had fought beside and against in equal measure. The man who had taught her everything she knew about holding a school together with sheer willpower.

"You're—" Her voice caught. She swallowed and tried again. "You're leaving?"

Schwartz nodded. "It's time."

Elizabeth's fingers curled into fists. She wasn't ready for this. Not now. Not when the ground beneath her was already shifting too fast.

He must have seen the war in her expression, because his lips twitched in something almost like a smile.

"I want you to apply," he said simply.

Elizabeth blinked. That, she hadn't expected.

"You're the only one who cares enough to fight," Schwartz continued. His voice was steady, but there was something else beneath it—certainty. Confidence.

In her.

That made her stomach tighten.

She wanted to say yes.

Wanted to grab onto the offer and never let go.

Because he was right—no one cared like she did. No one fought like she did.

But.

Can I lead a school while breaking the law to protect kids?

The thought sliced through her like a blade.

Could she stand in front of an entire faculty, demand integrity, enforce rules—while she was sneaking into houses at night, fighting men in the dark, taking justice into her own hands?

Could she be both?

Her silence must have spoken volumes, because Schwartz studied her for a long moment before speaking again.

"Maybe leadership isn't about perfection," he said, voice quieter now. "Maybe it's about doing what needs to be done."

Elizabeth's chest tightened.

That was it.

That was the thing that had been clawing at her since Craig died.

Because she had done everything right. She had followed protocol. She had gone through all the proper channels.

And Craig still ended up dead.

Because the system didn't work.

The system had never worked.

And now, she had a choice.

To keep fighting within the rules.

Or to reshape the rules entirely.

Her heart pounded.

She looked at Schwartz, at the man who had spent years leading this school with his sleeves rolled up and his fists clenched, fighting for kids in the ways that the system actually allowed.

And she thought about herself.

About the dark alleys, the bruised ribs, the late-night training with Abraham.

About the safe she still needed to crack, the girl she still needed to save.

Maybe she could be both.

Elizabeth straightened.

She met Schwartz's eyes, and this time, she didn't hesitate.

"Then yes," she said. "I'll apply.

Sixteen

The street was dark, the air thick with the scent of rain-soaked pavement and something rotting in the gutters.

Elizabeth crouched beside Ashley in the bushes outside Michael Carson's house, her pulse hammering against her ribs. They had planned this for days.

This was the last shot.

Michael had left twenty minutes ago. His car had disappeared down the road, taillights swallowed by the foggy night.

"We don't get another chance," Elizabeth whispered.

Ashley nodded. "Then let's move."

They slipped through the side yard, their gloved hands steady as they worked the lock on the back door. Elizabeth's fingers were quick, practiced from months of breaking into places she wasn't supposed to be.

A soft *click.*

The door swung open.

Inside, the house was silent. Dark.

No music. No TV. No hum of a refrigerator.

Just emptiness.

Elizabeth led the way, moving quickly but carefully, each step measured, each breath controlled.

They had minutes. Maybe less.

The safe was where Emily had said it would be—in the closet of the main bedroom.

Elizabeth knelt in front of it, pulling out her lock-picking kit. Ashley hovered behind her, keeping an eye on the hallway, fingers curled around the handle of a flashlight.

"Hurry," Ashley muttered.

Elizabeth didn't answer. She couldn't. She was too focused.

The tumblers shifted under her careful touch.

One.

Two.

Click.

She exhaled slowly and yanked the safe open.

The camera was inside, right where Emily said it would be.

A small black device, ordinary but monstrous, sitting atop a bundle of papers.

Elizabeth grabbed it. "We got it. Let's g—"

A creak.

A shadow in the doorway.

A voice like gravel and knives.

"What the fuck do you think you're doing?"

Michael.

Elizabeth spun, shoving the camera into her jacket.

Michael Carson stood in the threshold, his face carved from pure fury, his body tensed like a loaded spring.

And then—

He lunged.

He hit her like a battering ram, sending both of them crashing into the dresser. Elizabeth's back slammed against the wood, pain blooming through her spine, but she didn't have time to register it.

Michael's hands closed around her throat.

He was bigger, stronger.

But she was faster.

She twisted, bringing her elbow up in a sharp, brutal strike to his jaw. His teeth clacked together. He stumbled.

Elizabeth didn't hesitate.

She drove her knee into his ribs, sending him reeling backward, gasping for breath.

But he recovered too fast.

Michael grabbed a lamp from the nightstand and swung.

Elizabeth ducked, barely avoiding the arc of ceramic as it shattered against the wall.

Ashley screamed.

Michael's head snapped toward the sound.

Elizabeth took her shot.

She grabbed the closest thing within reach—a heavy wooden picture frame—and slammed it into the side of his skull.

The crack was sickening.

Michael grunted, stumbling. Blood dripped from a gash at his temple.

Elizabeth didn't wait for him to recover.

She grabbed Ashley's wrist. "Run!"

They bolted.

Michael roared behind them, the sound of footsteps pounding against hardwood.

Elizabeth reached the front door first, yanking it open, barely noticing the sting of glass slicing her palm from the broken window beside it.

They hit the street, running.

Didn't look back.

Didn't stop.

Not until they saw the flashing red and blue lights of the police station.

Only then did Elizabeth finally let herself breathe.

Seventeen

Elizabeth sat in the police station, her knuckles raw, her body aching from the fight.

The small interrogation room smelled like stale coffee and bureaucracy. Fluorescent lights buzzed overhead, flickering just enough to be annoying. She stared at the camera sitting on the metal table between her and Officer Smith, its black casing innocuous, ordinary—except for the evidence it held inside.

Smith inserted the SD card into his laptop.

Ashley sat beside Elizabeth, her hands clasped so tightly her knuckles had gone white. Neither of them spoke.

And then the video started.

The footage was grainy, but the horror was crystal clear.

A woman—Sarah Keller—stood in a dimly lit living room, her expression tense, exhausted.

"Michael, stop," she said. "You're scaring her."

The camera tilted as Michael Carson stepped into view. His movements were slow, deliberate, dripping with the same calculated control Elizabeth had come to despise.

A young Emily sat curled on the couch, small, trembling.

"Sarah," Michael said, voice low, dangerous. "You're overreacting."

"No," Sarah snapped. "I want you gone. I'm done."

Michael's face changed.

It was subtle—the tightening of his jaw, the darkening of his eyes.

Elizabeth's stomach clenched.

She knew that look.

She had seen it before.

Then—the screen went black.

A few moments later, the camera came back.

The angle had changed.

The couch was empty.

Sarah was gone.

And Michael?

Michael smiled at the lens before reaching out—

The video cut off.

The silence in the interrogation room was suffocating.

Officer Smith exhaled through his nose, his fingers curling into fists as he pushed back from the table.

"Well," he said, voice tight with restrained anger. "That's enough."

Elizabeth nodded, throat too tight to speak.

Smith stood, jaw clenched. "I'll have a warrant by the end of the day."

And just like that—

Michael Carson was done running.

The arrest happened hours later.

Elizabeth stood outside the school gates when she saw them—three squad cars, sirens off but lights flashing, crawling down the street like sharks through dark water.

Michael Carson was already inside the school, likely waiting to pick up Emily.

Officer Smith led the charge, his normally casual posture replaced with something hard, unyielding.

Elizabeth didn't go inside.

She didn't need to.

She stayed where she was, standing with Ashley, both of them holding their breath.

Minutes stretched.

Then—

Michael Carson was dragged out in cuffs.

His face was a mask of rage, disbelief, and something else.

Something dangerous.

His eyes found Elizabeth.

And he smirked.

Like he was telling her—You got me this time.

Elizabeth's skin crawled.

But then the officers shoved him into the back of a squad car.

And just like that—

It was over.

Emily's aunt arrived the next morning.

Elizabeth watched from a distance as Emily stood in front of the school, frozen, unsure.

The woman—a thin, red-haired woman in her early forties—rushed forward, eyes glassy with emotion.

"Emily," she whispered, kneeling down, arms outstretched.

Emily hesitated.

Then, like a dam breaking, she collapsed into her aunt's embrace.

Elizabeth turned away, blinking fast.

Ashley nudged her. "You crying?"

Elizabeth snorted, rubbing a knuckle against her eye. "Shut up."

Ashley smiled.

Because for once—

The system worked.

Because they forced it to.

Eighteen

Elizabeth sat in her car outside the bar, fingers gripping the steering wheel, her mind caught in an endless loop of uncertainty. She had made tough calls before. Had stood in front of raging parents, had filed CPS reports knowing nothing would come of them, had thrown punches in the dark against monsters who deserved worse.

But this? Breaking up with a good man? It felt unnecessarily cruel.

Rick didn't deserve this.

Her phone buzzed in the cupholder.

RICK: I'm inside. Can't wait to see you.

She closed her eyes briefly, exhaling the truth she didn't want to admit. Rick was a great guy—too great. The kind of man who showed up with flowers just because, who remembered the name of her favorite wine, who made space for her in his life without asking for anything in return.

And she had been using him.

Not in a malicious way, not intentionally, but…
he had been an escape. A warm bed on cold
nights. A steady presence when the weight of
the world felt too heavy.

And that wasn't fair.

Not to him.
 And not to her.

With a deep breath, she pushed the car door
open and stepped out.

Rick's smile was easy and familiar when she
walked into the dimly lit bar. He looked exactly
the same—button-down rolled at the sleeves,
relaxed, confident, happy to see her.

"Hey," he greeted, standing as she
approached. "You look good."

She forced a small smile, sliding into the seat
across from him. How the hell was she
supposed to do this?

She wasn't a woman who fumbled for words.
She handled angry parents, emotional
students, difficult staff meetings with precision
and control.

But now? She felt like a coward.

She stared down at the condensation forming on the untouched water glass in front of her.

Rick studied her, his expression shifting as realization set in. Something was off.

"What's going on?" he asked, voice gentle but firm.

She inhaled, lifting her gaze to meet his. No more hiding.

"I can't keep pretending this is something it's not."

Rick frowned, leaning forward slightly. "What are you talking about?"

Elizabeth swallowed. Just say it.

"You don't really know me," she admitted, her voice quieter than she intended. "Not all of me. And I need someone who can love the whole picture—even the part that hides in the dark."

Rick's lips parted slightly, his brows drawing together. "Elizabeth—"

She held up a hand. "You deserve someone who isn't constantly compartmentalizing. Someone who isn't keeping secrets or sneaking out in the middle of the night. Someone who doesn't... doesn't thrive in the chaos the way I do."

Silence stretched between them.

Rick's throat bobbed as he swallowed, his fingers curling into the edge of the table. "I care about you, Elizabeth."

"I know," she said softly, her chest aching. "That's why I can't do this anymore."

She could see the wheels turning in his head, the way he was trying to find a way to fix it, to argue, to convince her that whatever she thought was wrong could be right again.

But there was nothing to fix.

This wasn't about love or attraction.
It was about compatibility.
And they weren't.

Rick ran a hand through his hair, exhaling sharply before nodding—accepting.

"So… this is it?" he asked.

She nodded once. "Yeah."

They sat there for a moment, both absorbing it, both knowing this was the right thing even if it hurt like hell.

Then, slowly, Rick stood.

Elizabeth followed.

They hesitated for half a second before stepping into an embrace that felt final but not bitter.

"I hope you find what you're looking for," he murmured against her hair.

She closed her eyes briefly. "You too."

And just like that—
 They let each other go.

Nineteen

The morning was cool and crisp. The scent of freshly cut grass drifted through the air, mingling with the faint chemical tang of asphalt after an early morning sprinkler run. Somewhere beyond the gates, a lawn mower hummed in the distance, its steady drone fading beneath the chatter and laughter of students filing onto campus.

Elizabeth stood just outside the front entrance, arms crossed, weight balanced evenly despite the dull ache in her shoulder. Her knuckles were still scabbed over from the last fight. Beneath her pressed blouse, bruises ghosted along her ribs, reminders of every hit she'd taken, every lesson she had learned.

But she stood tall.

She always did.

A group of students passed by, oblivious to the battles fought just days before. Oblivious to the fact that their assistant principal had broken into a house, had fought a man to the death— or near enough—just to protect one of them.

It struck her, suddenly, how much she had changed.

Before, she had fought within the system. Filed paperwork, made reports, followed procedures. She had believed, maybe naively, that the right words, in the right order, to the right people, would create change. That the system—flawed as it was—could be fixed.

But it couldn't.

It never could.

Because the system was never built to protect the ones who needed it most.

And if the system wouldn't do it, she would.

She caught movement from the corner of her eye.

Emily.

The girl was walking alongside her aunt, who had flown in from Maine just days ago. Elizabeth noted the way Emily held herself—lighter, freer. The tension in her small shoulders had eased, though it would take years for her to truly untangle everything Michael had done to her.

She wasn't broken.
Just healing.

Their eyes met briefly, and Emily offered a small, tentative smile.

Elizabeth nodded back. A silent promise.

She would be okay now.

Elizabeth turned, stepping back toward the school entrance. Her heels clicked against the pavement, sharp and deliberate.

For years, she had felt like she was drowning, trapped beneath an ocean of bureaucracy, injustice, and helplessness.

But now?

Now, she was awake.

Now, she had a new purpose.

She wasn't just an administrator.
She wasn't just another cog in the machine.

She was a protector. A force of nature.

She was Elizabeth fucking Kane.